Snowbird Christmas

Vol. 2

Holiday Stories to Warm Your Heart

Edited by Nancy L. Quatrano

Printed ISBN: 978-0-9854381-5-9
Kindle ISBN: 978-0-9854381-4-2

Copyrights © 2013 by Suzanne Baginskie, Sharon E. Buck, Dianne Ell, Audrey Frank, Jackie Grommes, Richard Hébert, Daria Ludas, Susan Paris Lyle, Patricia Marinelli, Nancy L. Quatrano, Mark Reasoner, Cheri L. Roman, Drew Sappington, Wilma Shulman, Claire Sloan, Anita S. Taylor, Elaine Togneri, and Judy Weber.

Copy editing by Daria Ludas, Cheryl Johnson-Konrad, and Nancy Quatrano

Interior, front and back cover design by Jonni Anderson and Nancy Quatrano

Interior layout and pagination by Jonni Anderson (www.StarWatch-Creations.com)

WC Publishing

an On-Target Words company
4625 Cedar Ford Blvd.
Hastings, FL 32145
ontargetwords.com/wc-publishing

What readers had to say about the 2012 Snowbird Christmas Collection:

Contents

Contents, Cont'd

from the Editor

Dear Reader,

Once again, a talented, generous, and wonderful group of authors have joined me to present another volume of Snowbird Christmas, a collection of Christmas-based short stories offered to bring more peace, joy, and love into the world!

This 2013 volume shares twenty new stories from some of the same authors in Volume 1, but there are also a good number of new authors with fun adventures, characters, and locations real and imagined. I've had a wonderful time reading and editing this year's contributions, and again, I was moved by each and every one that is in the book.

All of us wish you a very Merry Christmas, one filled with happy memories, laughter, and peace. May this year's celebration of the birth of Jesus Christ kindle that spark of God's love that will light up your life.

Best wishes, always.

Nancy L. Quatrano, Editor

The Season's Crowning Touch

Suzanne Baginskie

Two weeks before Christmas on a lazy Saturday afternoon the phone rang. My husband Al's employer called and offered him an out of the state job transfer. Wooed by a hefty bonus and promise of eternal sunshine, balmy breezes, and palm trees, he accepted. Our plans of decorating the artificial tree and draping lights over the home's rooftop eaves all changed. Instead, we packed several boxes and scheduled our furniture to be shipped to a rental home on Florida's west coast.

Al squeezed the last suitcase into the back compartment, and our family of four climbed into the minivan for the long ride. We departed as the first blizzard of New Jersey swirled down from the cloudless gray sky and bid us a chilly goodbye. Al hunkered over the steering wheel and glued his gaze on the icy road ahead. Each time the wipers struggled to clear the wet, clingy snowflakes from the windshield another pile took their place.

Once we hit Maryland, we merged onto I-95 and joined the snowbird traffic headed south to spend their winter months in a warmer climate. My six-year old daughter Christine and my four-year son Alex had fallen asleep. When they woke up an hour later, they bombarded me with questions.

"Mom, when will we be there?" Alex asked.

"We have to stay overnight at a hotel, so late tomorrow afternoon."

"Can Dad stop? I need a bathroom break?" Christine said.

"Sure, we're almost out of gas," Al said and grinned at me. He pulled off at the next exit.

"How will Santa ever find our new house?" Alex said.

"Santa knows everything," I answered and gritted my teeth. How could I convince my two young children that he would have no problem finding them? The nearer we got, images of unpacking, buying groceries and preparing for the holiday season hung heavy on my heart. It all sounded so overwhelming. I wiped a tear off my cheek and tried not think about the close family and friends we'd left behind.

The next day, guided by the female voice on the GPS, we coasted into the cement driveway of our new house. Everyone rushed from the minivan. Hot rays of the Florida sun and dense humidity welcomed us. I gazed at the home's front yard. The loose gravel, sand and clumpy weeds washed away the "tropical paradise" I had envisioned. Two hours later, the furniture arrived.

It took a few days to settle in and finish the unpacking. My bored daughter sat on the couch and gazed out the glass sliding doors.

"Mom, when's it going to snow?"

"It doesn't snow in Florida. Rain, yes, but there won't be any snow."

"But Mom, Santa's sleigh won't be able to land," said Alex. A look of sadness appeared on his young face.

"He'll find a way, lots of other children live here," I said softly.

My heart pinged. Vivid memories of wishing for

a snowfall on Christmas Eve would become a thing of the past. The glittery white flakes enhanced rooftops, trees, and bushes and always created a winter wonderland glow. I knew the kids would miss snow as much as I would.

Sunday afternoon, I browsed the newspaper and noticed a craft store had a sale on canned artificial snow. I could purchase several and embellish the windows. I smiled, but kept this a secret.

"Al, I'm going shopping," I told my husband. "Keep an eye on the kids."

"Okay, be careful," he answered.

Unfamiliar with the local area, I programmed the GPS to gain access to the main roads. As I cruised along, I enjoyed all the ornate decorations and potted red and white poinsettias gracing homes and town businesses. Florida's warmer weather allowed festive displays, and many windows and outdoor trees blinked with red, green, and yellow lights.

When I reached the highway, I blended into traffic and listened to Christmas carols on the radio. I remained in the middle lane, unsure of my next turn. Climbing a small hill, my car's steering wheel seemed to lurch right. I glanced at my speedometer and applied the brakes. My speed was ten miles over the limit.

On the hill's downside, I slowed even more and gazed at a tall, chubby Santa waving at passing cars. I raised my hand, but he swung around and pointed at the SUV ahead of me. A uniformed officer motioned the vehicle to the curb. Disguised as Santa Claus, he and the other policemen were issuing traffic tickets. No holiday spirit here. I turned the radio's volume louder, "Rockin' around the Christmas Tree" blared. Singing along, I pressed the gas to the beat of the rhythm and unknowingly sped up again.

A voice behind me whispered in my ear, "Jane, slow down."

I gasped and stomped the brake pedal. The wheel jerked right once more. I decreased my speed, signaled, and veered over a lane. Spooked, my heart pounded hard inside my chest. I glanced in my rearview mirror. I was alone in the car.

A massive squealing of tires pierced my eardrums. On the other side of the highway a blue sedan had accelerated. The driver must have lost control because he spun toward the median and skidded across all three lanes striking two passing cars. The sedan flipped twice and slid sideways on the asphalt. Sparks flew from beneath the steel body as the car ground to a stop two car lengths in front of me.

I panicked, swerved the wheel right, and steered into a parking lot. Stunned, I loosened my seatbelt and switched off the ignition. What had just happened? My hands shook and my pulse raced.

A pick up truck drove in and parked next to me. The driver bolted from his vehicle and rapped on my window. I peered out before lowering it.

"Are you okay?" he asked as he stared at me.

"Yes," I whispered. "I am."

"What made you slow down like that? If you hadn't, both you and I would have been in that car's path when it crossed the median."

"I'm not sure, but I heard a voice tell me to slow down," I muttered.

He studied me, searching my face for answers. "Thank God. I was going too fast with all the hustle and bustle of the season. Merry Christmas to you and your family," he remarked. He walked back to his vehicle and drove away.

Should I go home? My sense of security had deserted me. Had I just experienced a miracle or maybe the voice of a guardian angel? Something made me avoid that accident. I glanced around to find my bearings. There stood the Hobby Lobby craft store. What a coincidence

— or was it? I thought of my children. I climbed out on rubbery legs and wobbled in through the front door.

Two hours later, I finally arrived back home. When I told my husband what had happened he said, "It's all over the news. I prayed you weren't anywhere near it." He hugged me, his warmth and concern radiating reassurance.

I told him about the angel's voice. I really believed she was perched on my shoulder and had whispered in my ear.

On Christmas Eve, we tucked the children into bed and read them "The Night Before Christmas" poem. Afterward, Al helped me frost all the outside windows with the cans of artificial snow. When we finished, we stood back and admired how the fluffy white flakes sparkled under our colorful lights. Minus real snow, I'd found a way to give our home a winter wonderland glow.

Tired, we went inside for a cup of hot cocoa. Al tuned in the late night news. The television weatherman announced a cold arctic air was blowing south all the way into Florida. Temperatures would drop into the fifties overnight. I smiled. We'd have a slight Christmas chill.

The next morning we plugged in the lights, lit some logs in the fireplace for ambiance and sipped mugs of coffee. When the children awoke they dashed into the living room.

"Wow, Mom. Santa did find our new house," Alex said. His brown eyes widened.

"Look at all the packages under the tree," Christine said. "A bigger pile than last year."

Al's huge bonus check had come in handy. He winked at me.

"Our stockings are filled to the top," Alex said.

"See, I told you Santa wouldn't forget you," I said. "He has a magical sleigh and twelve speedy reindeer, so he's able to fly all around the world."

"Look Mama, he brought us snow too," said Alex, his

cheeks flushed as his tiny fingers pointed at the white glistening windows.

"It's so beautiful, Mommy. Even prettier than last year," Christine said.

Warmth flooded me. I vowed to spray the windows again next year. As I watched my children unwrap their gifts, I silently thanked that special angel for delivering me home safely.

She was the holiday season's crowning touch.

About the Author

Suzanne Baginskie has sold several fiction and non-fiction short stories. They appeared in fifteen *Chicken Soup for the Soul* anthologies, two *Cup of Comfort* books, *The Wrong Side of the Law* anthology, Woman's World magazine, two Daily Flash fiction books and several True Romance magazines and various newsletters.

She belongs to Mystery Writers of America, Florida Mystery Writers, Florida Writers Association and Sisters-in-Crime. Visit her website at http://mysite.verizon.net/resv100m.

The Gift Bag

Sharon Buck

She slowly opened the brown grocery bag with hands gnarled and twisted cruelly by the ravages of arthritis.

"What's this, honey?"

The voice I so dearly loved was old, wavering, and yet still full of hope with a tinge of surprise. She looked up at me with those tired blue eyes and a hint of a smile on her lined face. Tenderness and love radiated from her. I wanted to memorize every wrinkle on her face. I wanted to lightly run my fingers over each and every one of them. I wanted to tell her I was sorry for the pain I had caused over the years. I wanted to tell her how much I loved her but the words wouldn't come out. I didn't want this to be the last Christmas we shared. I couldn't let her see me fall apart.

Why? I don't know. Maybe it was because I couldn't admit to myself how much I really did love her. Maybe it was because I would have to open my heart and see the love that truly existed between us. Maybe I was just scared she would die too soon. Any time would be too soon. I wanted her to stay here on earth forever. I wanted her to stay with me forever. Even eighty-five years was too short a time. I couldn't imagine my Christmas, my Easter, my birthday or any other day of the year without her to share it with.

I cleared my throat. "It's from BJ at church. She said you had to follow the instructions on the list," I said as I pulled a sheet of paper out of the bag. It was typed in large bold letters and triple-spaced so aging eyes could easily read it.

"Could you read it to me, please? I'm a little tired." She lay back on the pillows, watching me lovingly and carefully.

As nice as this rehab facility was and as kind as the staff was to my mother, I didn't want this to be her final remembrance of life. I wanted to take her home where she could see her day lilies, the yard, the trees, the birds flittering to and fro and the squirrels trying to sneak up the bird feeder to steal food. I wanted her to be in her own home. Maybe it was just selfish of me or maybe that's just what I needed to believe for me. But, this wasn't about me.

"Well, the first day you are to tell each of your daughters one funny thing you remember about them."

She shut her eyes, her face peaceful; she smiled, and then giggled.

"Do you remember when you were in kindergarten and we lived in Lake City and we were driving and you wanted to know how fast ten miles per hour was because you thought it was fast?"

I laughed. "Yeah, I remember putting my head in your lap so I could see through the steering wheel how fast it was. The guy behind us kept honking his horn at us and then finally whipped around the car."

We both laughed.

"Hand me my cell phone so I can call the girls later." It didn't make any difference which of my sisters my mother called. We were always "the girls."

"I love you, Mom.," I said, kissing her gently on the forehead. "See you tomorrow."

I prayed I would see her tomorrow. She had a bilateral pulmonary embolism — large blood clots in both lungs. The doctors thought they had probably come from a severe brain bleed and emergency brain surgery she'd had several months earlier. It was still touch and go with her because of trying to get the Coumadin levels correct. Too much, my mother's brain would start to bleed out, too little and it could create more blood clots. Either way, death was hanging on the doorstep.

Though she wasn't home for Christmas, day after day she slowly got better. Each day she eagerly looked forward to BJ's gift bag to see what delightful treat was in store.

One day I asked if BJ had been in to see her.

"No, BJ doesn't come to hospitals, nursing homes, or shut-ins."

"Really? Why not?" I was puzzled.

"I don't know, honey. I've talked to her a couple of times on the phone and told her how much I appreciate the gift bag. She says she just can't come to visit." My mother's eyes were much clearer, much more alert. She smiled, "I understand, honey, and it's okay."

After a couple of weeks of rehab, the Coumadin levels finally stabilized. Delighted, I was able to bring this tiny little old lady, whom I loved with my entire heart, home. She had made a miraculous recovery and the doctor felt sure she would continue to have a long, healthy life.

I ran into BJ about a week after New Years at the local coffee shop. As usual, she was in a hurry and ready to scurry out the door.

"Hey! Sit down just a minute, girl, nothing's that important!" I grinned and waved at an empty chair.

BJ was one of those ageless women who could have been anywhere between fifty-eight and eighty with red hair just this side of being gaudy, yet fashionably young.

She was always twitching as though a tiny jolt of electricity ran through her to keep her revved up.

"Thank you so very much for the gift bags for my mom. It meant the world to her."

I searched for the right words to say and then decided to just speak from my heart. "I honestly think it helped her to get well and to come home." My eyes welled up with tears. "Thank you so much, BJ. I can't begin to tell you what she means to me."

BJ just sat there for a moment and then the professional smile came out. "No problem, my dear. I was happy to do it. Just part of my church work." She started to get up.

"Where did it come from? Where did it start?" Still seated and clutching my coffee cup, I just looked at her.

She slowly sat back down. "You know, no one has ever asked that." She kind of laughed, more out of sadness than fun. "All these years, no one has ever asked me that."

She sat for a moment, her eyes starting to glisten with tears. She quickly reined them back under control.

"Our family was in France in World War II and we were trying to get back to the U.S. It was tough. The bombings, the lies, deceit; food was scarce, it was awful. I was young, very young."

She paused and took a sip of her coffee. "My father had finally found a way for the four of us to get back to the U.S."

She looked up. "You know, I never did know what my father did for a living. Anyway, it would be fifteen days before we could leave. We were all very excited.

"So my mother, knowing that we would bug her to death with "is this the day we're leaving" questions decided to make up a gift bag with something for us to do, appreciate, see, or tell each day. So every day we would pull out something from the brown sack she had and then we would do it. It was fun and certainly kept us occupied."

A tear splashed from her perfectly made-up eyes into her coffee cup.

"Our last morning in France, we were so excited because that was the day we would leave to go back home to the United States."

She was quiet for a moment and then, composing herself, continued. "Some type of mortar roared through the house and hit both of my parents, killing them instantly."

She discreetly dabbed at both eyes with a tissue.

"The guy my father had made the arrangements with to get us to the U.S. found us and took my brother and me to the cargo ship. I really don't remember much about the trip.

"We finally got to the U.S. and my grandparents took us in. There were two large duffel bags that had been with us. My brother and I didn't open them for years."

Her eyes no longer focused, glazed over at the memory.

"One day I looked inside the then-rotting duffel bag and there was the brown paper sack that my mother had put our daily gifts in."

At this point, BJ reached out her hand and I took it in mine. I no longer made any pretense of trying to keep my tears from flowing.

"The last gift my mother left in the bag was a handwritten note." She smiled self-consciously. "The last thing in everyone's gift bag is a self-addressed stamped envelope to me. The gift bag is a tribute to my mother."

BJ looked up and smiled through her tears. "Her last note to me said, 'BJ, I love you more than you will ever know. Love, Mom.'"

About the Author

Sharon Buck is a speaker, an author, and senior book marketing consultant who coaches other authors to create a national platform to ignite their book sales. She has had five books published and is currently at work on her first fiction novel. Her websites are www.BookAuthorsTour.com and www.OffTheShelvesFast.com. She can be reached at Sharon@BookAuthorsTour.com.

After All These Years

Dianne Ell

The night the robbery took place at the Hamilton mansion, the house was filled with guests, the temperature was in the low seventies, and it was Christmas Eve. In Palm Beach, Christmas was referred to as high season. The time when the city was glutted with celebrities, dignitaries and ordinary visitors. It was also a time when parties were non-stop which meant homeowners were extra vulnerable from thieves.

On that night, the Hamilton's fifteen room house was a showcase for Christmas cheer. A floor to ceiling tree decorated with silver angels, and white candles graced the living room. The grounds were aglow with white lights. And Christmas music filled the air.

Each Christmas Eve, as they had done for as long as anyone could remember, Victoria and Gerald Hamilton hosted a dinner where family and friends convened to share a glass of wine or brandy and to toast the start of the holidays. Dinner was buffet style enabling guests to enjoy the house, the pool area, the formal gardens, or the veranda overlooking the ocean.

There was nothing extraordinary about the night. No uninvited guests. No one drinking more than they should. Victoria Hamilton wore, as she usually did, her legendary Mayan Fire, as the necklace was known. Her husband had brought it back years ago from an expedition to the Mayan jungles where he had gone with a team from the museum. The necklace, made of intricate links of gold with a huge emerald surrounded by diamonds as its centerpiece, was supposedly worn by a Mayan queen.

Not feeling well, around ten thirty Victoria went to the bedroom. She took off the necklace and laid it on the dresser. She planned to return it to the safe which was in the dressing room camouflaged by closet shelves and cabinets in the morning.

That year, the Hamilton's daughter Marlene, her husband Jason Stanton, and their two daughters Devon, seventeen and a senior in high school, and Alexis, twenty and a journalism major at the University of Florida were staying at the mansion between Christmas and New Years.

Two days after the dinner, late in the afternoon, Victoria Hamilton was getting ready to attend a museum event. She went to where the necklace was kept and found it missing along with other pieces from her jewelry collection.

The police were called in immediately. The house was searched and an investigation began.

During the high season, the Palm Beach police encountered many robberies, and during the years, about ninety per cent of the thieves were caught. The Hamilton case was going to be their nemesis — at least for the next twenty years.

Present Day

Alexis Hamilton Stanton placed the laptop on the footstool, got up from the sofa and stretched her back.

Writing for a living was hard...on the back, the knees, the circulatory system, and after a while, on the fingers. She was only forty and already arthritis was setting in.

Working on what she hoped was her tenth bestselling mystery, she picked up her cell phone, laptop and mouse and headed for the library where she had a view of the Intracoastal Waterway. It was mid-afternoon in mid-December. A time when shadows began to stretch across the lawn of her Deerfield Beach home and long rays of the sun captured islets of light on the blue surface of the Intracoastal. So focused on writing she had missed lunch. In her gleaming, renovated kitchen, Alexis made a turkey and ham sandwich, grabbed a bag of sour cream and onion potato chips, an iced tea, and headed for her library.

Settled into a comfortable chair, she ate her sandwich as she scrolled through her email. She had a note from her sister Devon who was now chasing spies across Europe with the CIA. Since her move to the Continent and her marriage to a Frenchman, she rarely visited the States. The note said it was time to put everything to rest and she would land at Palm Beach on the twenty-second of December, a week from now. Could Alexis meet her flight? Alexis replied that she had been thinking the same thing, and yes, she'd be at the airport.

Each year, just before Christmas, some journalist, resurrected the tale of the theft of the Mayan Fire. The police had never found the culprit nor the missing jewelry. This year was the twentieth anniversary. Amazing how time has flown, Alexis thought.

The puzzling aspect of the theft was how well her grandparents had taken the robbery. It was her parents who'd felt the effect. Her mother blamed her dad for the loss, accusing him and some of the unsavory people he did business with. Her dad said the same about her mother and her friends. And with that, they ended an unhappy twenty-two year marriage. Her mother now lived in southern California. Her father remained in Miami with the business. They had both remarried.

Victoria and Gerald Hamilton were around and doing well. Gerald remained active in local politics and various charities. Her grandmother continued to paint and have showings at local galleries. While Devon hadn't returned to the Palm Beach house in twenty years, Alexis, if she wasn't traveling, was there.

The email reminded Alexis of a meeting she had had with her grandmother two weeks earlier. They had had lunch at a restaurant on Worth Avenue. It was nice to see her grandmother but she was still puzzling over some of the conversation.

"I received a call from the magazine section of the Post wanting to do a retrospective on the theft of the necklace. I said no as I always do, but I was wondering if you planned to write anything on it. It is the twentieth anniversary." Her grandmother, although in her mid-eighties, drove a Maserati, looked mid-sixties, and was still quite a lovely woman. Impeccably dressed as were most of the people of Palm Beach, she looked at Alexis with curiosity.

"I hadn't planned to," Alexis answered. "Do you think I should?"

"Goodness, no. But with all those mysteries you write, I wanted to make certain I hadn't missed anything on the subject."

"You haven't. And if you get a call again, send them to the Palm Beach police. The statute of limitations has run out on the theft. No murder was involved. If there were any suspects they've long vanished. But if someone in the department's been following the case, maybe they'll find a story that way."

Her grandmother smiled warmly. She reached across and patted Alexis' arm, light radiating from her jeweled fingers and wrist. "I'll pass that on."

On the hour drive back to Deerfield Beach, Alexis

thought about the lunch. She hadn't mentioned Devon's visit. Maybe her grandmother knew. She'd always had that kind of radar.

Back home, she found a voice mail from Major Dan Greenley of the special crimes unit. She and Dan dated occasionally. Others hoped for more.

"Have an unexpected lead in the necklace theft. Call me."

A lead after twenty years? It sent a chill up her back.

They met at The Cove on the Intracoastal. After hours for Dan, he was casually dressed in khakis, a polo, and a navy blue sports jacket. With his sandy hair and blue eyes, it would be hard to recognize him as a Major with the Palm Beach County major crimes unit. He smiled at her but this time, no kiss. This is serious, Alexis thought.

They sat on the deck near the railing. The setting sun cast long shadows across the water where boats prowled and anchored. It would be dark soon.

"Did you know your grandparents hired a private eye to investigate the theft?" He opened his briefcase and removed a folder. "For you."

"I didn't know." Alexis took it and quickly glanced through it. Where was this going?

"I got a call from Interpol last week. It had to do with the theft. Apparently, a piece from the collection has shown up after all these years. And since I never knew much about the case, I decided to look into it. I read the police reports, but that is much better." He pointed to the folder. "The detective did a good job. Better than our guys."

"Probably because he was unencumbered by politics."

"He was certain it was an inside job."

"I heard that." Alexis looked out at the waning light. She didn't like how the conversation was shaping up...

"The call from Interpol was about this." He removed an ivory silk packet from his jacket pocket and handed it to her.

Alexis lifted the flap and stared. Glared was more like it. Damn. How did this happen? No wonder Devon decided it was time. The pin, a flamingo created with rubies for the body and yellow diamonds for the beak and legs, had been part of the jewelry taken along with the necklace. It was on the list her grandmother had given to the police. Alexis lifted the bird and ran her finger over the jewels.

"Who had it?" It was difficult but she looked him straight in the eye.

"Came from Monte Carlo. A man tried to pawn it. The shop owner identified it as made by Tiffany in Palm Beach. The numbered piece was still on Interpol's list of unrecovered gems. The man confessed he stole it from an apartment in Paris. Your sister's apartment."

Alexis leaned against the back of the chair refusing to show surprise. "And you've talked to Devon?"

"She's been unavailable."

"She's coming for Christmas. You can speak to her then."

He nodded. Sipped his beer, then leaned forward. "You and Devon took the jewelry." He searched her eyes looking for confirmation. "Why?"

She hadn't expected the question to be so direct. "Inside job doesn't mean my sister and I did it."

"Explain the flamingo." He looked at the pin.

"Grandmother gave it to Devon."

"A ten thousand dollar pin to a seventeen-year-old?" Even in the dim light she could see his skepticism.

"Devon liked it. End of story. Ask my grandmother. "

"It was on the list she gave the police. Was your grandmother's necklace insured?"

"I don't know. Why would I know that? Maybe my mother would."

"If it was insured, she never put in a claim. Which comes full circle to you and Devon taking it, and her sitting patiently until you returned it. Isn't it about time?"

He reached for the pin at the same time Alexis dropped it into her handbag. "It's going back to the rightful owner. The French police can deal with the thief. And nowadays, the pin is worth a hundred thousand, not ten.

***

Devon, her long straight hair touching her shoulders, stood beside her sister Alexis in their grandmother's closet. They unlocked the safe, and from the brown bag where they had stored the jewels ten years ago, they began replacing them in the exact order in which they were kept. Everything was in place except for the necklace.

"Dan Greenley knows we took it?" Devon asked.

"He wanted to know if it was insured."

Devon shrugged her shoulders. "Why does he care?"

"I have no idea."

Devon was still holding the necklace when the door to the closet opened.

"It's about time," their grandmother said. She was wearing the same green silk gown she had worn on that Christmas Eve long ago.

Devon sighed. "Oh. We are so, so sorry." Her eyes filled with tears.

"We are," Alexis nodded. "It was a game. A stunt. We thought the police would solve it. But, they didn't. Time passed and it became harder and harder to say it was a joke. And then a year passed, then five. And here we are." Alexis looked at her grandmother helplessly. "I'm sorry for the anguish we caused you and granddad."

"The only real casualty was your parent's marriage," Victoria Hamilton stated. "And it turned out to be for the best. They were never right for each other." Then her expression softened. "The real gem of the marriage was you two."

"And you still feel that way?" Alexis asked.

"Of course." She put her arms around both girls.

"When did you know we'd taken it?" Alexis recalled the recent lunch.

"Not right away. But when the detective said it was an inside job, we ran out of suspects except for the two of you. From the earliest age you both were always looking for crimes to solve. And when there weren't any, you'd create them. Devon went on to become a spy, and Alexis, you write about them. But ... the coup de grâce ..." she looked at Devon "...was a photo you sent. You were wearing the flamingo pin. It's unmistakable. A one of a kind designed by Tiffany."

Devon sighed. "Alexis said that taking it would get me into trouble some day. But I always liked that pin."

"Do you still have it?"

"Yes," Alexis interrupted, taking the silk packet from her pants pocket and placing it in her grandmother's palm.

She hadn't told Devon about Dan returning it. "You can thank me another time," Alexis said to her sister, who had a most incredulous look on her face.

With Devon still holding the necklace, their grandmother walked over to a nearby drawer and opened it. She took out another necklace and put it on. "This is the real Mayan Fire."

"Then what did we take?" Devon looked at her grandmother.

"A duplicate. We had it made the moment Gerald brought it back from the expedition he went on. Cheaper than insurance."

"But you've never worn it since that night ten years ago." Frown lines crossed Alexis' forehead.

"How could I? Then I'd have to admit that the necklace had a duplicate. While everyone does that, the museum might have started questioning everything we ever donated. Couldn't have that."

"We stole a fake?" The sisters stared at each other.

"Serves us right," Devon said.

"How are you going to explain the necklace?" Alexis asked.

"A Christmas present from a considerate and gracious thief. Come, let's go downstairs."

In the living room, the ceiling-high Christmas tree glimmered with silver angels and white lights as it had that Christmas Eve of ten years ago. The temperature was in the seventies but logs burned in the fireplace. Poinsettias filled the open spots around the large room. special Christmas music filled the air. Time stood still.

Her grandfather opened a bottle of champagne and poured four glasses. "Christmas brings out the best in people." He looked at the necklace and held up the glass.

"You have been more than patient with us," Devon said. "And again, we're really, really sorry."

"Did the jewels ever leave the house?" their grandfather asked.

"No," Alexis replied. "They were in the second floor library in a special metal box."

"Then there was no theft," their grandfather said. A smile spreading across his face. "To all's well that ends well. Merry Christmas. "

About the Author

Dianne Ell has written for trade and consumer publications, online magazines and websites. Her previous suspense novel, The Exhibit was a TOR/Forge publication. Her short story, "Last Man Standing" will be published by Sherlock Holmes Mystery Magazine. She is a member of the Mystery Writers of America, Author's Guild and FWA.

A Christmas Feeling

Audrey Frank

It was a cold, dreary night and Peyton Taylor was alone. She loved St. Augustine, but even the millions of twinkling white lights in the Plaza across from the Cathedral didn't cheer her. It was the second year she'd been widowed and memories of Fred flooded her thoughts. They had always done things together. She thought she had adjusted to life as a widow but, for whatever reason, she was haunted tonight.

She started to walk to her car. From the corner of her eye she saw an older gentleman with a short white beard. He waved at her as he came from the Cathedral. Of all things, he was wearing a Santa Claus hat. Strange attire for someone who must be in his mid-sixties.

His walk was brisk as he crossed the Plaza. His cap bobbed up and down.

"Excuse me for approaching you this way, but I watched you during the service. You looked so sad. Is there anything I could do to help?"

Peyton shrugged. "Just the Christmas blues. It'll pass. Thank you for your concern, though.

He smiled and his eyes twinkled. "Could I at least offer you a cup of coffee at the pub around the corner?"

Why not? she decided. When they were inside, hot black coffee warming her, he introduced himself.

"I'm John Webster." He reached across the small table.

"Peyton Taylor." She took his hand.

He had a trusting, jowly face. Without the Santa hat, she saw bushy white hair that matched his beard.

He sipped his coffee and asked how long she had lived in Florida.

"Just a year. When my husband died two years ago, I needed to get away from New York and Fred and I used to visit here on vacations. I was scared to death to leave all I knew to start over, but I felt it was something I had to do. I opened a small shop on Aviles and live in the upstairs apartment. It's small and sort of Bohemian, but I have a nice balcony where I can enjoy the night air after a busy day at work."

"I've lived here all my life. Married my college sweetheart. Never had the urge to leave."

A frown flitted across Peyton's face. "My biggest regret is that I don't see my children very often." She wiped at eyes that, against her will, filled with tears.

John touched her hand. "Do you like Christmas lights? I know a lot of people who own houses that are gloriously decorated. Would you trust me to drive you around to look at them?"

She hesitated only a moment before accepting his invitation. Christmas lights had always enchanted her. They left the pub and he pointed to his Lincoln. Holding her elbow, they crossed the Plaza. Next thing she knew they were off and running.

They wove through paved and cobblestoned streets where he pointed out elegant houses. He explained about the people who lived there. Many friends had passed over or moved away, but several of the friends he had grown up with were still there.

The old Victorian houses sparkled like jewels. Open porches were covered with lights that dazzled the eyes, their large columns wrapped in deep green pine garland and holly boughs. Large Christmas trees glistened with hand-blown glass ornaments. As they drove past one house, John stopped the car and got out. He waved to a couple who were on the front steps.

"John, old man," the woman called out. "Come join us for some eggnog."

John bent down and peered at Peyton. "Okay with you?"

She nodded and found herself inside, where a glass of strong, homemade eggnog appeared in her hand. John explained they could only stay a few minutes. He had a lot more he wanted to show Peyton. After hugs and calls of "Merry Christmas" they were on their way again.

John continued down the winding, narrow streets, pointing at certain houses, explaining about the people who lived there. It was like driving through spun sugar. Peyton was lost in the glow of magic John provided. St. Augustine wasn't such a tourist mecca when he was a teenager and he was such a gifted story teller, she could picture the old city just the way he described it.

"We didn't have the traffic problem we have today. I could ride my Schwinn all over town without worrying I'd be hit by a car." He slowed the car on Marine Street. "Look over there. She's magnificent, isn't she?"

Peyton looked where he pointed. A large schooner was anchored in the bay. Its sails gleamed with white lights. A tree was decorated on the deck. She felt herself smile, her heart felt a little lighter.

"I always wanted to go sailing," John said. "My wife couldn't swim and had no intention of learning, so I never bought a boat. Think it's too late now?" He cocked a bushy eyebrow at her.

Peyton giggled. "Somehow, John, I figure you can do

anything you want. Age has nothing to do with you." She reached over and lightly kissed his cheek.

They had driven around town for over three hours and this stranger had become her friend. He said he'd be coming to see her at the store once the holidays were over.

"I'd like that," she admitted.

He drove her back to her car where they said their goodbyes. Watching him leave, Peyton could swear she heard him exclaim as he drove out of sight, "Merry Christmas to all and to all a good night."

About the Author

Audrey has been writing for more years than she can remember and is an author and short story writer who resides in the St. Augustine, Florida area. Her novella, *Under Margret's Wing*, is currently available at Amazon and Kindle. Her website is www.audreyfrankauthor. com.

The Christmas Table

Jackie Grommes

The humble little family was meant to have a grand dinner table like other families in the village. It had been a difficult year fraught with problems and unexpected surprises. Baby Luke cooed in his hand-made wooden swing next to his sister Emily, only a year older. Luke didn't know his swing had first belonged to his sister, just that she could stare into his eyes which made him smile and that his mother could gently push him and start him rocking once again. Yes, there were surprises but welcome ones nonetheless.

Luke's father, Gabriel, had recently lost his job at the mill. The work could be seasonal and this year he had been laid off just before the holidays. He kept himself busy because he was very handy with wood and the home was full of whittled toys and other pieces made from scraps of lumber he had brought home with him when he was still working.

Gabriel and his father, Quinton, were making plans to build birdhouses to sell at craft fairs next to antique chairs and delicately embroidered linens. These would not be ordinary birdhouses. On his solitary walks through the woods behind their house and on trips to the beach, Gabriel had collected "pieces and parts" as he liked to call them — small scraps of fallen birch, gnarled wood roots that spoke to him, acorns, tiny bits of moss. The beach yielded unique shells others might have walked right past because of imperfections. These treasures would become the jewelry of the birdhouses, draw the eye, and captivate patrons as they walked through the faire.

Gabriel had no aspirations to become famous for his artistic talents, although his mother thought he should be. Gabriel's art came from deep within his soul and he couldn't help the creations that bubbled up inside him and spilled out. When he was a young boy, his mother brought home a collection of fabric scraps and left them in her sewing room to turn into placemats and aprons. The next morning she had found her son asleep on the sofa in her work room. On the rug was a tapestry that covered nearly the entire floor made from the scraps. Brilliant colors and patterns had been carefully placed and created a breathtaking work of textile art. It was as though a village of women had worked for months to create the stunning piece instead of her brilliant son who slept, satiated, now that his vision was before him.

But now, Gabriel was a man with a growing family to think about. One day he went to Quinton and asked for his help making a table for their kitchen. The budding family demanded a gathering place for meals and he wanted to provide one. He hoped to have it completed for Christmas dinner. His mother had discovered a perfectly good table at a sale in town but it was too ordinary for his special family. Instead, he produced odd scraps of wood he had gathered on his walks around the winding roads near his home and in the scrap pile at the mill. He positioned them carefully on the large work table in his father's shop. To the untrained eye they were random pieces of wood in various sizes. But, to Gabriel they represented so much more. This would become the place his family gathered to share their meals and discuss the details of the day as they came together in the evening. He worked methodically and soon the table began to take on the final pattern as he had envisioned it in his mind's eye.

There the unfinished table top lay. Each time father and son looked at it, they agreed that it was beautiful but needed something unique to set it apart and make it truly amazing. Perhaps they would varnish it a distinctive color, Gabriel suggested. Another idea was to apply decorative hardware. But none of those ideas seemed sensible so they continued to walk around and around the table hoping a vision would materialize and help them decide how to finally finish their special piece.

The table top was temporarily forgotten when the family learned that they would be visited by Gabriel's uncle, Finley. They hadn't seen each other in several months and they were all very enthusiastic about such an exciting deviation from their normal daily routine. Quinton and Finley had a lot in common because they were both experienced wood workers. They were well thought of since master craftsmen of the day had a greater than average intelligence, mechanical aptitude and were competent in geometry. Many could read technical drawings if required. Together, they held many years of experience as well as a shared discrimination in choosing only the finest woods.

After they greeted each other enthusiastically, Quinton and Finley set about updating each other on the family news and vowed not to let so much time pass before they saw each other again. They lamented getting older and not being able to do all the projects they wanted to. Years before, Finley had built an entire kitchen while his family cooked on an outdoor stove and ate on a makeshift table, but the wait had been entirely worth it. His carpentry skills were impeccable and the magnificent cabinets were the showpiece of the kitchen. Carefully crafted from the finest Heartwood Maple, the cabinets gleamed from hours of sanding and polishing. Finley had chosen his wood carefully with an artful eye and the fine woodwork was stunning. He was pleased to hear about his brother and nephew building a table and he agreed that they shouldn't take short cuts on their project.

A few days after Finley returned to his home in the neighboring village, a large carton arrived via a rumbling rural delivery truck. Quinton was astounded to receive a package from his brother whom he had seen only a few days before. He produced the knife from his belt and carefully opened the crate which revealed the most beautiful and unique piece of wood Quinton had ever seen. His specialized eye immediately recognized the wood as Sinker Mahogany.

Sinkers had been under water for over 100 years in Central American countries before they were retrieved, and even small selections were highly valued. The pattern on the small square was more exquisite than any he had ever seen. Quinton knew that the piece was very old because the reddish hues in mahogany deepen with time. Once he could take his eyes away from his new treasure, he saw that a note was attached written in Finley's scrawling handwriting.

I harvested this from Grandfather's old tea table and have been saving it for a special project. I would be proud to see this piece of our family history in your table.

Deepest regards, Finley

Father and son were astonished and very grateful. They seemed of one mind about how to use the treasured piece of wood in their table. An inlay was created in the center with the prized specimen. They turned it at an angle so that the inlay made a dramatic geometric statement in the large heavy piece. Both men agreed that the table was now perfect. They sanded the raw wood rhythmically until it was flawless. The table was eyed from every level and light to make sure nothing was missed. Final protective coats of varnish were applied so as not to mar the handsome finish with glass rings and children's spills. When the varnish was dry, the grains of the mahogany and maple rose in the wood and came to life.

The table was ready for the celebratory Christmas dinner. Finley was invited to share in the celebration. The grateful families pooled their resources so that they might have a magnificent dinner worthy of the prominent new table. Great platters of brown sugar ham and sweet potatoes waited to be devoured. Steaming preserved vegetables harvested from the summer garden glistened with butter. Gabriel's sourdough rolls accompanied his wife's delicious cooking. Grandmother's china was brought up from the cellar for the first time in many years and made a respectable showing next to the polished brass candelabra with flickering red candles.

Two high chairs were positioned next to each other on one side of the table and Gabriel took his rightful place at the head surrounded by the people he loved so deeply. The difficult times of the past year were forgotten. So important was this special meal that Gabriel had written down his prayer so he wouldn't forget any of the words. Even the babies sensed the significance of the occasion and were unusually quiet. Gabriel pulled the folded paper from his pocket to read as the family joined hands.

He looked around the table at his beloved family. "Bless us, oh Lord, and these thy gifts, which we are about to receive from thy bounty..."

About the Author

Jackie moved to St. Augustine, Florida to be near family and discovered the FWA group one Saturday. Rubbing elbows with so much talent rekindled her love of writing. Her story "Going Home" was published in The Florida Writer/Spring 2013. She has a few short stories in the works and then plans to return to her real love, children's story books.

Jason's Gift

Richard Hébert

Jason watched from the parlor window as the boys raced their go-carts down the hill. He stood back from the curtains, not wishing to intrude on their play. Soapbox cars, he thought, shaking his head as if to banish the thought. We called them soapbox cars. Now they were calling them go-carts. This was 1949. The Second World War had ended but a few years ago. Just one more sign that the world was heaving with change. Soapbox cars, thrown together from household scraps — a crate, a board, some carriage wheels — were evolving into "go-carts."

A half dozen boys age ten or so raced by yet again on Pine Ridge Lane. Why they had named it that he never had understood. There wasn't a pine tree or a ridge anywhere in sight. It was just your standard suburban one-block-long hillside road, without lane markings or even a sidewalk. Just a hillside crossed by a strip of unmarked pavement.

Johnny from across the street ran Billy off the road into the weeds just below Jason's property line. Billy fell off in a flailing heap as his cart capsized. The others gathered around, howling and slapping their thighs like monkeys. Billy didn't seem to mind. In fact, he joined in. After all, for this moment, the overweight boy from up-hill was the center of attention. This was how the boys of Pine Ridge Lane played on school-year weekends, now that the real war was over and they had put away their toy guns.

Jason's son stood silently apart from the others, at the mouth of the driveway uphill from the merriment, as though guarding his home against merriment's inva-sion. Jason believed he understood why: his boy didn't have a go-cart. In this place and at this time, a go-cart was essential to a young boy's self-esteem, a significant stepping stone to the day he would be 16 and drive a real car.

Go-carts are boys' introduction to ownership of "wheels." Sure, they had tricycles and wagons and even scooters and bicycles before the go-carts came along, but those were toys, not vehicles they had fashioned with their own hands, the way soapbox cars had been made for decades. Toys might bring movement; go-carts brought pride.

In those days before Go-Karts — with a capitalized "G" and "K" — had motors and roll-bars and sped on spe-cially-designed tracks, before they looked and screamed like miniature NASCAR racers, young boys raced their homemade carts — with a small "c" — on hilly streets like Pine Ridge. Their carts were simple, constructed of three- or four-foot planks riding on four wheels, typi-cally from discarded baby carriages, and mounted with an upended crate for a hood. The front wheels were fixed to a swiveling cross-bar that served as both footrest and a steering device that responded to a rope tied to each end. In effect, the rider steered with both hands and feet, especially useful if, say, you wanted to ram someone like Billy off the road, or avoid getting rammed yourself.

The go-carts were light, built for speed. The trick was to push the cart as fast as you could run and leap aboard at the last possible second before momentum and gravity took over. After that, it was all in the steering and the swiftness of your wheels.

***

Pine Ridge Lane extended only one block, lined on either side by a handful of houses. It was ideal for cart racing because of both its sparse traffic and its slope — flat at top and bottom but steeply inclined much of its length. In a few weeks, when the snows would come, the local children would put away their go-carts and switch to sleds, that is until the snow plow came, or the dreaded sand truck. But this was late autumn and the hill was still dry, perfect for go-cart races. Cars that approached respected this and gave the boys right-of-way.

Watching them tow their carts back uphill, hardly noticing his son at the driveway as they passed, Jason knew what he would give his son for Christmas, a go-cart that would convert him from outcast to the envy of the others. Not that his son had ever voiced a desire to have what the others had. He was a bookish lad, and whether for Christmas or a birthday, the only gifts he ever asked for were books. Books about horses. Or dogs. Science books. Science fiction books. Anything about the stars.

But Jason preferred that his son be more down to earth like the others, more rough and ready to mix it up with them, more competitive, prepared to defend himself and his honor when challenged, no longer the outlier, the onlooker.

"My boy thinks too much," he'd told himself often enough that it had become a mantra. He'd never dared utter, even to himself, the uneasiness that fathered the thought — "He will be hurt by life" — but that was what he feared, without knowing quite why.

***

Now that The War had been won and the soldiers had come home, Jason's son proudly wore his Uncle Roger's jacket to school every day, a jacket just like the one General Eisenhower wore in every picture he'd seen of the man. He even carried his schoolbooks in an official U.S. Army khaki canvas knapsack given to him by "Lefty," a family friend who had served in Europe and come home with only one arm — his left.

The son understood that these things linked him to something important that had happened on the other side of the ocean. He had yet to learn the details other than that it had involved a lot of fighting and killing, and that everyone was glad it was over, but he knew it was something to be proud of. Jason had taken note of his son's pride in his mementos of The War. That was why he resolved to build him a World War II Army jeep go-cart for Christmas. Let Irene buy him more books if she wished. Jason was going to see to it that his son would have a go-cart he could drive with pride.

Jason was manager of a small mill that trafficked in the detritus of the textile industry, processing the ends of bolts of cloth, bobbins of thread and the left-over cotton waste the mill sold to the makers of mattresses and car seats. Each evening, he stayed in the mill's tool-shop an hour or two after work designing and building the finest go-cart ever owned by a young boy.

With a jigsaw he shaped sheets of particleboard into side panels, a seat-back and a hood. He mounted two flashlights on the hood and tacked a red leather cushion to the seat, raised a few inches off the floorboard. What other boy owned a go-cart with "headlights" and such a seat, let alone one that was cushioned? He even rigged a proper steering wheel that gave the driver greater control. No light-weight go-cart would ever ram this jeep off the road.

The wheels presented a problem. The vehicle was too heavy for baby-carriage wheels. He settled instead on spare steel wheels from the supply room, next to the great hall where the cotton bales were stacked. Rails ran the length of the hall's ceiling, and steel wheels rode the rails dangling chains with grappling hooks to carry bales to the loading dock at the railroad tracks. No one would miss the four wheels he fitted to the jeep go-cart.

On Christmas Eve, Jason carried the go-cart home in one of the mill's tractor-trailer trucks, the cart safely hidden from view under a tarpaulin. Nothing unusual there. He often used a truck from the mill as his own transportation, one of his perks as manager. Christmas morning, with temperatures in the mid-fifties and the roads still dry, he led Irene and his son, all wrapped in their bathrobes and new slippers, out to the truck. Then he backed the jeep down a ramp and set it before the boy. A giant red bow was tied to the steering wheel. His son looked up at him in confusion.

Jason grinned. "It's yours. Go ahead. Try it out." Then, still seeing confusion in the boy's eyes, he said, "It's a jeep go-cart. A jeep, just like they had in The War."

Jason helped push the cart to the crest of the hill. The boy climbed aboard, tucked his bathrobe about him, and gripped the wheel fiercely. As Jason pushed from behind, the jeep rumbled into motion. Slowly it gathered into itself the momentum of Jason's pushing. Then, seconds after it was released careening downhill, the jeep coasted slowly, hesitantly to a stop. It waited there in the middle of the road, half-way down the slope, with its bewildered driver. This go-cart was built for war, not racing. It was far too ungainly for coasting.

Jason had to push the cart back uphill from behind because the boy couldn't pull it alone. His son's disappointment showed on his face. Tears welled in the boy's eyes and broke Jason's heart. They parked the go-cart jeep at the back of the garage. It would never go out again.

§ § §

I never thanked my father for that jeep go-cart. I'm certain he saw the disappointment in my face. I made no attempt to hide it. What he couldn't know, because he died only a few years later, when I was still too young and callow to understand the measure of a father's heart, was that I learned in due time what he'd given me was something far more precious than a steel-wheeled go-cart. That cart was a token of his love.

Merry Christmas, Dad. And thank you.

About the Author

Richard Hébert, a former award-winning investigative reporter for *The Atlanta Constitution*, has authored both fiction and nonfiction books, national magazine features and documentary films. Now residing in St. Augustine, Florida, he writes a political blog, "Richard's Take," at www.richardhebert.com. He can be contacted at rlhebert0906@att.net.

Silver Bells

Daria Ludas

"Rosa, I know it's Christmas Eve, but it's a new job." Ricardo Lopez hugged his wife. "You know how lean things have been. I finally get a job after all these months and you don't want me to go in? Mike said he would pay me time and a half to work Christmas Eve."

"I'm preparing your favorite dishes and your parents will be here shortly." His wife wiped a tear with her apron. "Do you have Ricky's tricycle put together?"

"Yes. It's in the shed. Once he's asleep, my dad can help you get it." He jingled the coins in his trouser pocket. "At least we will have a little more cash for Christmas."

He put a comb through his hair, fastened his name plate to the silver shirt and turned to his wife. The door bell rang.

"I'll get it," young Ricky yelled as he pounded to the door of their modest mobile home. "Maybe it's Santa, for me!" He opened the door and looked around outside to see his grandparents standing there. "Oh, it's *la abuela y el abuelo*," he said softly. "I mean, grandma and papa."

They hugged and kissed him as he squirmed. "Merry Christmas, Ricky," they said in unison.

"Where's Santa?" he asked.

Ricardo, Rosa and both grandparents looked at each other.

Ricardo took his son to the couch and they sat together. "Son, it's too early for Santa. You have to be sleeping for him to come. "

Ricky nodded his head, smiling. "He will come and leave me a new bike."

Rosa Lopez hugged her son. "We will see what he brings, okay?"

"I know he will come. Cowboy Santa with the silver bells is coming."

"Who is that?" Ricardo asked with a laugh.

"He is Santa and he wears a cowboy hat. He has a big silver car and rings silver bells after he leaves the toys."

"Your mama told you not to make up stories, Ricky."

"It's not a story. The kids at preschool told me about him. Some of them got toys already from him. They said he rings bells after he drops a toy on your porch." Ricky ran to the window and shoved open the curtains. "I know he is coming here tonight."

Ricardo hugged his son. "I have to go to work. Give me a kiss. Your grandparents are going to stay the night and spend Christmas Eve with you and mom." Putting his son's feet on the floor, he ruffled his dark curls. "You be a good boy and go to bed when your mama tells you."

"I promise I will." Ricky glanced at his mother. "Mama said you might have to go to work tomorrow, too. Do you?"

Ricardo looked at his wife, and then to his son. "I don't know about that yet. But I promise you, I won't be there too long." He kissed Ricky on the forehead. "I love you, my son. Go to bed early so Santa will come."

He kissed his wife and his parents, and went out the door. He lingered on the front porch for a moment, and gazed up at the stars. "Thank you, Lord, for this new opportunity for my family." He scurried to his old Jeep and drove away.

Ricardo parked in the crowded lot and walked into the Silver Belle Lounge. Every seat at the horseshoe bar was occupied. Servers scurried about to deliver food to crowded tables.

Mike Regan swung through the office bat-wing doors. "Hey, Ricardo!" Mike shook Ricardo's hand and grabbed his shoulder. "Boy, am I glad to see you, buddy."

"Call me Ric, Mike. Sorry I'm a little late. Christmas Eve — the family, you know." Ricardo said.

"I know. I'm sorry to ask you to come in, but I think of you as my right hand around here, Ric." Mike waved his hand around the place. "You're the manager and it's becoming a happening place. That's why I hired you. I needed someone I knew I could trust and manage a busy place. Your hotel management experience was just what I needed — lucky day for me when you applied for this job."

Ricardo could feel his face warming. "Thank you. I will always do my best for you."

A blonde woman wearing a plunging neckline and Christmas ball earrings sashayed over to Mike, and dangled mistletoe above his head. "Merry Christmas, Mikey," she purred, and kissed his lips.

Mike hugged her. "Merry Christmas, Meredith."

Ricardo grinned as she sauntered away. "Girlfriend?"

"No. We dated a few times, but I date other women, too."

"No special lady in your life?"

"Not these days." Mike's smile turned serious. "I was engaged for a long time to a smart and pretty girl in New Jersey. Two days before the wedding, she dumped me. She said I worked too much, and was more concerned with making money than paying attention to her. I had to cancel the ceremony and reception."

"Sorry man. That's hard." Ricardo patted Mike's shoulder. "I didn't mean to pry about your love life."

"It's okay. I left Jersey, headed south and stopped when I got over the Georgia/Florida border. Looked around and bought this place. Took me a while to renovate it, but here we are."

"Glad to be part of it, Mike. It looks successful right now."

Mike shrugged. "Doing okay. How about you? Did you get your son that bike you were telling me about?"

"No. We couldn't afford it right now. We got him a refurbished one. My dad painted it red for him, but it's just a tricycle. We're hoping to get him the bigger bike for his birthday in March. He's a bit small for what I wanted to buy him, anyway."

Mike nodded, then turned and disappeared into the kitchen. Ricardo leaned against the bar and looked around. A few minutes later, Mike reappeared wearing his leather jacket and a grey Stetson.

"Ric, I have a few things to take care of. I'll be back in a few hours. You're in charge, buddy."

Then Mike walked out the front door.

"Ugh!" Sandra, the bartender yanked the handle on the tap and poured two glasses of foam. "Damn!" She breathed deeply, took two new glasses, and pulled the tap. Amber beer flowed into the glasses and she set them on the tray.

Ric walked behind the bar. "Everything okay back here?"

She wiped her hands on the bar towel, avoiding his eyes. "He has some nerve, walking out on us when it's so busy." She swept back the curls that had fallen across her forehead. "Things to take care of. Right. More like, what lady is he taking care of?"

Ricardo sighed, then smiled. "Do you want a break? I'll cover for you." He served two glasses of Pinot Grigio to the couple at the far end of the bar.

"Thanks. I'll take a break in a few minutes. It's just that the past few weeks, Mike has left here every night at peak hours to take care of things, with goodness knows who, and we're stuck doing all the work."

Ricardo wiped down the granite bar. "But that's why he hired us. Right?"

"Maybe." Sandra blushed.

"Maybe it's more? You kind of like Mike?"

"I wouldn't mind dating him. I mean, what single female wouldn't?

He pointed to an empty table in the bar area. "Go take your break, have a bite to eat. Relax a little bit. I'll cover things here."

"I am angry. Do me good to cool off, I guess." Sandra removed her apron and placed it on the shelf. "Holler if you need me."

***

The silver Escalade pulled into the Prestige development and stopped at houses which had Tot Finder medallions in the window.

A man got out at each home, placed toys on the front porch, and sounded bells before he drove off. The man reached 38 Ridge Road, the Lopez home, and left a shiny red, two-wheeled bicycle on the porch.

The bells rang as the silver Escalade sped away.

Young Ricky burst through the front door, and discovered the bike. "He was here, he was here! See? I told you!"

Rosa dashed through the open door. "Ricky, come inside right now. It's too late to be out here." Her in-laws followed her.

"I knew he would come. I heard the bells. Santa brought me just what I wanted." Ricky climbed on the bike.

"Where did that come from?" Mr. Lopez asked.

Rosa shrugged. "I really don't know." She gently removed her son from the bike. "Let's bring it inside now, and put it by the tree."

Rosa, Ricky and Grandmother went inside. Grandpapa rolled the bike into the house and placed it next to the brightly lit tree. He glanced at his wife and daughter-in-law, then shrugged his shoulders and winked.

"Let's get you into bed, young man. You must go to sleep now, Ricky. Maybe Santa will bring you more things."

Ricky smiled. "Santa doesn't have to bring me anything else. I have my new big-boy bike." He kissed his grandparents and scurried up the stairs to his bedroom.

Rosa tucked her son under the covers. "Say your prayers now. Tomorrow we will celebrate the birthday of Jesus. That is the true meaning of Christmas, remember? Good night."

Rosa returned to her in-laws who sat in the living room. "What excitement, yes? How about some chamomile tea to help us sleep?"

"That sounds good. I will put on the water," said Mother Lopez.

"Rosa," Grandpapa called. "What will we do with the tricycle that is in the shed?"

"When Ricky is sound asleep, we will bring it out, too." Rosa knew how much work and love her father-in-law had put into the tricycle. "That new bike is too big for him right now. His feet couldn't reach the pedals. He can ride the little one until he grows into the two wheels."

Grandma Lopez brought a tray with Christmas cups and her famous fruit-filled cookies and placed them on the coffee table. "Let's enjoy this quiet Christmas Eve, yes?" she said with a twinkle in her eyes.

***

The Silver Belle Lounge closed to customers at eleven. Ricardo, Sandra and the rest of the staff were busy cleaning and polishing the bar, tables, floor and kitchen.

Mike strolled in about eleven-thirty. He placed his hat and jacket in his office, and returned to the lounge area.

"Folks, you did a bang up job here tonight — the joint was jumping! You've all worked hard, so go ahead home. I'll take care of the rest of this."

Sandra narrowed her eyes. "You're not opening tomorrow are you?" she asked.

"Well, here's the thing. I thought I'd open up for a couple of hours. Don't want anyone going hungry on Christmas, do we? But it's just going to be take-out orders. So, just come in from noon to two."

"It's Christmas Day, Mike. Everyone wants to spend it with their family," she said as she reached for her jacket.

"No problem. Bring your families. They can hang out here with you. It's only a few hours, and hey, I'll pay you all double time."

The staff looked at each other, and then nodded.

"Be back here at noon, sharp."

***

Half-past midnight, Ricardo walked into his house. "Merry Christmas, Rosa" he greeted his wife, who was dozing in the chair. He noticed the large red bike next to the tree. "Where in the world did that come from?"

"No one knows," Rosa said. "Our son insists it is from Cowboy Santa with the bells.""Did he see him?"

"No. But he heard the bells. He was looking out the window all evening. The bike is a little big for him, so he can ride the tricycle for a while." She smiled at him. "You're not working tomorrow are you?"

"Yes. But only a few hours, and I can bring my family

with me. So all of you can come, meet everyone, and see how nice the place is."

She sighed and pushed herself up out of the chair. Then she took his hand in hers. "Okay. If that's what we have to do to spend the whole Christmas Day together, then that's what we will do."

Christmas Day at noon, the Lopez family entered the Silver Bells Lounge, along with several other families. Ricardo was speechless.

Each table was covered in a green, red, or gold linen tablecloth with silver napkins.

Poinsettia centerpieces graced each table. A bountiful buffet of holiday foods was set on the bar.

Mike greeted Ricardo's whole family. "Ric, Merry Christmas." He bowed to Rosa, Ricky, and Ricardo's parents. "Welcome. *Mi casa, su casa*," he said, then escorted them to a table.

Mike served glasses of champagne to the adults and ginger ale to the children. When all were settled in their seats, he clinked a glass with a spoon.

"I just want to thank my staff for such a successful four months. There's no work for you today or tomorrow so you can spend time with your families. Please raise your glasses for a Christmas toast."

He cleared his throat and looked around the room. "To my staff — my new family — and all of your families, a Merry Christmas." He put his glass on an empty table and spread his arms wide. "Please help yourselves. The buffet is ready."

As Mike went into his office, Ricardo followed and closed the door. "Thanks, Mike."

The big man turned around, a wide smile on his face. "Ah, don't mention it. I wanted to celebrate with the staff. You're all my family now."

"Yes, well thanks for that, too. But I meant thanks for the bike."

Mike gazed downward. "What do you mean?"

"I know who you are — 'Cowboy Santa with the bells.' That's what the kids around here call you anyway."

"Don't give away my secret, Ric. I don't want people to know, especially the staff."

"So that's what you've been doing the past few weeks? People here thought you had hot dates."

"No, not so lucky. Just trying to make some kids happy."

"Well, you've done that, *mi amigo*."

Mike's face was bright red. "Listen, Ric, I need your word that you'll keep my secret."

Ricardo nodded. "Tell you what. I'll keep your secret if you get to know Sandra better. I think she might like that."

Mike frowned. "You sure about that? She's always scowling at me."

"Trust me, she'll like that."

Mike extended his hand. "Okay, buddy. It's a deal."

Ricardo grinned as they sealed their agreement. "Come. Join us at my table. We're sitting with Sandra and her mother."

Mike pulled a chair next to Sandra, placed mistletoe above her head and kissed her cheek. "Merry Christmas, Sandra."

Sandra blushed from her feet to her face. "Merry Christmas, Mike," she whispered before she returned his kiss.

Ricardo looked at Rosa, who gave a slight nod. "Say, since we're eating here today, and we're closed tomorrow, why don't the two of you come to our house for dinner?"

"Thanks, Ric. Consider it a date," Mike said.

Young Ricky smiled at everyone. "And I can show you the two cool bikes I got for Christmas!"

"We'd like that, Ricky," Mike said, putting his arm across the back of Sandra's chair.

"We'd like that a lot."

About the Author

Daria Ludas resides in New Jersey with her husband of forever. Recently retired from many years as an elementary school teacher, she's looking forward to writing full time and working with her husband in their real estate business.

She's a member of Sisters-in-Crime and Liberty States Fiction Writers and is published in several crime fiction anthologies with her short stories.

Too Busy

Sue Paris Lyle

I spent the entire morning rearranging the merchandise at the major department store where I work. Every day before Christmas is like this. Our store manager is happiest when we're moving things around. He always says, "People have to see it to buy it!"

I was topping off a trio of female mannequins with some brightly colored knit caps when I saw my sister, Ann, and her son enter the store. Waving, I called out to them. My five year old nephew, Zander, was rosy-cheeked with excitement because we were going to have lunch at the food court and then see Santa.

"Are you sure you have time for lunch?" Ann asked, giving me a quick hug. "You look busy."

"Oh, these girls can wait," I said taking a couple of straight pins from my mouth so I could talk better. "Besides, this time of year I'm always..."

"Aunt Carrie! Aunt Carrie!" Zander attacked me with a surprise bear hug around the knees, nearly knocking me over. He looked up with big grin.

"Hi Zander," I said rubbing my hand over his curly

brown hair.

"Come on, Aunt Carrie!" said Zander releasing my legs and tugging on my hand.

"Zander, can't you see that Carrie's busy?" Ann gave her son an exasperated glance. "When she's finished, we'll go to lunch."

My nephew looked disappointed, dropped my hand, and pushed the toe of his sneaker into the floor. "Okay — grownups are always busy."

"Zander," I said, gently touching his shoulder so he would look at me, "as soon as I pin this last hat on I'll punch out, get my purse, and I'll be ready to go."

"Don't rush," said Ann looking down at her son and pulling him close. "Zander and I will go look at Christmas decorations."

A few minutes later I found my sister looking at tree toppers and Zander in front of a table top display of miniature nativities. A few weeks ago I had arranged the display of three different crèche scenes so customers could see what they looked like out of the box. One was intentionally primitive, carved from teak, another was made from brightly painted resin, and the third was cast from delicate porcelain. Each came with a simple barn-like structure, an array of animals, and complete set of figures.

As I walked up to Zander I noticed he had a confused look on his face. I watched as he glanced all around the table top, and then on the floor.

"Zander," I said, "What's wrong? Did you lose something?"

"No, Aunt Carrie," Zander said seriously. "But something's missing."

Concerned, I squatted down next to Zander and put my arm around his waist. "Sweetie, what's missing?"

"Jesus," he said pointing to first one nativity scene and then the next. "The baby Jesus is missing — there's no Jesus anywhere!"

"Oh," I said at a loss for words.

"How come there's no Jesus?" Zander asked, his little eyebrows pulled tightly together. "Everybody else is here — even the Wise Dudes."

"Wise Men," I corrected.

Zander stared at me unfazed. He only wanted answers. "Where's baby Jesus?"

"Well," I stammered unsure of how to explain why the baby Jesus was missing from each nativity scene. "He's still in the box — we didn't put Him out this year."

"Why?" asked Zander.

"Because when we put the baby Jesus figurine in the manger, He disappears."

"Like magic?"

"No, not exactly," I said looking into Zander's wide and innocent eyes. I was still struggling with how to explain shoplifting, a concept as foreign to my nephew as it would be to the baby Jesus. "People just take him."

Zander's eyes flew open with surprise. "That's stealing!"

"I'm afraid so."

Zander scowled like a detective on the case, threw up his hands, and shrugged. "Who would steal Jesus?"

"I'm sorry to say, most of the store employees blame little children like you."

"I wouldn't do that," Zander said with alarm. "It's wrong to steal."

I gave him a reassuring hug. "Yes, I know you wouldn't steal. Most little children know it's wrong to steal. That's why I think it's grownups who take Jesus."

"Why would they take Jesus?"

"I don't really know, honey."

"In Sunday school, Miss Carlene teaches us that Jesus is everywhere." Zander flung his little arms above his head and made a sweeping motion in the air. "Don't grownups know He's all around us?"

"I think a lot of times, especially when adults get too

busy, they forget that Jesus is with them."

"Is that why they take the baby Jesus?"

"Probably."

Zander gave a very adult nod of his head. "They want to feel the baby Jesus in their pocket so that they know he's close by."

I looked at my nephew with wonder. How could a little boy be so wise? He understood completely. While little children have no trouble believing that Jesus is always with them, adults need something more tangible — they have to see it to buy it!

Aunt Carrie," said Zander still looking concerned.

"Yes."

"Are you too busy for me?"

"Oh, Zander," I said taking his hand. "I'm never too busy for you — let's go eat!"

About the Author

Susan Paris Lyle is an artist, teacher, and writer/producer of four short films. In 2011 she received a Masters of Fine Arts in Contemporary Writing from Savannah College of Art and Design. She is currently finishing edits on her first murder mystery. Susan lives in Savannah, Georgia, with her artist husband, two useless dogs, and three indifferent cats.

The Christmas Train South

Pat Marinelli

What if I'd never taken that train? The thought struck me as I lugged my heavy baggage through the door of Auto-Train compartment One Twenty-three and looked around.

Four years ago today, and compartment One Twenty-three is *just* as I remember it.

***

It had all started after Mom and Dad retired and I headed to Florida on the Auto-train with Dad's vintage car trunk filled with Christmas gifts. I'd booked a sleeping compartment because with my job, I never knew if I'd need to catch up on sleep. Good thing since I'd just come off a thirty-seven-hour hostage negotiation and managed to be the last car loaded on the train.

"Anything else, Mr. Morgan, sir?"

"No thanks, I'm good. Looking forward to a good night's sleep." I pulled a bill from my wallet and tipped the porter who had prepared the upper bunk in the sleeper compartment for me. "And, Merry Christmas."

"If you need anything else, sir, just ring." The porter left. I stashed my Green Bay Packers' sport bag in the closet and climbed into bed.

When I awoke at six-thirty, I climbed down from my bunk. I needed a shower and a shave, badly. Later, while wiping off the last dredges of shaving cream, I opened the bathroom door and saw a woman curled up on the sofa seat, sound asleep with a heap of papers scattered at her feet. Loose curls of strawberry-blonde hair splayed across a pink fluffy robe draped over a black Pepe Le Pew nightshirt. My first thought was Santa came early and brought me one heck of a present. Second thought was, how did she get in here and when had she arrived? Then reality hit. This was every cop's worst nightmare, sexual harassment charges that could ruin a guy's career and put him in jail. She appeared innocent enough until her eyes popped open and a terrified expression took over. Not good.

Staying put with both arms raised in a 'hold it' position, I said, "Good morning, Goldilocks. Whacha doing in my compartment?"

Her mouth closed on the scream I knew almost made it out.

"It's my compartment," she said looking indignant and rang for the porter.

Glancing at my watch, I counted aloud, "Four, three, two, one," pulled a tee shirt over my head and waited—not long—for the knock on the door. "That'll be the waiter with breakfast." I pulled a bill from the inside pocket of my brown scruffy, leather jacket hanging on the doorknob.

"Come in," I said opening the door. The porter arrived at the same time. Goldilocks had stuffed all her papers in a briefcase and now stood, arms crossed over that tantalizing tee shirt, beside the sofa.

"You rang?" the porter asked.

"This is my room," the woman said as the waiter

handed me the breakfast tray. "What is he doing here?" she asked the porter.

"Mr. Morgan is booked here also, Miss Shanahan. Aren't you traveling together?"

"No," we both said at the same time.

I dove into my scrambled eggs. I figured as long as the porter was here I was safe, and I hadn't eaten since noon yesterday. I could use my negotiating skills, but hey, let the man do his job. I'm on vacation.

"May I see your tickets, please?" the porter asked.

I grabbed mine from my jacket while Miss Shanahan reached into her organizer for hers.

The porter studied both tickets. "Josh Morgan, compartment one twenty-three. Megan Shanahan, compartment one twenty-three. You're both ticketed for this compartment. You didn't book them together?"

"No," Megan cut in. "We don't even know each other. Could you please get him out?"

"That's not going to happen. I paid for my ticket, too." Well, Dad had paid since I was bringing him his precious convertible, but she didn't have to know that. "I'm not leaving."

"Can't you find him another compartment?" Megan asked.

"Sorry, ma'am. There are no empty compartments on this train. Booked solid for the holidays. This *is* the last train to Florida before Christmas. Best I can do is check if there's an empty seat available."

"Well, he can't stay here," Megan said.

"I can't explain the mix-up, Ms. Shanahan, Mr. Morgan," the porter said. "You each paid for a reserved sleeping compartment. You'll have to share the space, just for a few hours. We're due in Florida this afternoon. Keep the door open for safety, miss. You can report the ticket-issue error when you arrive." He read our tickets again and shrugged his shoulders. "Sorry but there's nothing I can do. Truthfully, I wouldn't even count on an empty seat."

"Wait!" cried Megan, pushing past me as the porter left. "You can't leave me in here with a strange man." But the porter continued down the aisle as if he hadn't heard her.

That's when I put myself in her place. Even with the compartment door open, I started to feel sympathy for her. So I did the next best thing. Hit speed dial on my cell phone.

"Hi, Mom. I need a quick favor. Please tell the young woman I'm sharing a compartment with on the train I won't hurt her and that I'm an okay guy... Long story, Mom. I'll explain it when I arrive. The lady's pretty shook up... Thanks. Here she is..." I handed Megan the phone.

"Hello?" Megan said, and then she listened for a long time.

What the heck was Mom saying to her?

Finally, she laughed, clicked my phone shut, and handed it back. "Do you feel safer now?"

She ignored me, but I thought I saw a smile trying to sneak out at the corner of her mouth.

"Do you mind if I sit on the seat facing forward?" I asked. "I really can't ride backward. It's a motion sickness thing."

"Fine." She gathered her organizer and a stack of papers and moved to the other seat. Having three sisters, I knew 'fine' was not a good thing. I poured another cup of coffee from the pot I'd ordered. "Want coffee? There's plenty. Rye toast, too."

"No thanks, I'm not much for breakfast, and I drink tea." She pulled a carry-on from the closet. "Would you mind leaving while I change clothes?"

It wasn't a question. "So you can lock me out? No way. I'll turn my back and look out the window. That's the best I can do."

"Fine. Just stay on your side."

That time, 'fine' took a sharper tone. Looking away, I

heard her rummage through her suitcase. The bathroom door slammed. That went well...not!

After finishing the rye toast and filling my mug with the last of the coffee, I rang for the waiter. He took the tray and brought a pot of tea for my companion. And then the train slowed to a stop in the middle of South Carolina. Not good.

"Why are we stopped?" Megan asked stepping from the tiny bathroom dressed in worn, faded jeans and a sweatshirt splashed with a Christmas tree design under which slept a huge white cat waiting for Santa. Tiny Christmas wreathes dangled from her ears. Someone had lots of holiday spirit. I like that.

"No idea, but I ordered you a pot of tea."

"Thank you," she said and glanced at the open compartment door. She poured a cup of tea and settled into her seat. "Your mother tells me you're one of the good guys. A cop."

"Detective. Robbery/Homicide. D.C. Metro. You?"

"Freelance editor. Boston."

"That would explain the stack of papers."

"This time. I wanted to get as much work completed as possible so I can enjoy the holidays in sunny Florida. I prefer paper to editing on a computer. Impossible on the waterfront in the sunshine which is my favorite place to be in the summer time. So, of course, I get a paper manuscript in December." She laughed.

I liked her laugh. Damn, I liked *her*.

"Where are you headed in Florida?" I asked.

"Crystal River. You?"

"Homosassa Springs."

I wanted to continue the conversation, but Megan picked up the manuscript and started working. She pretended to ignore me, but every once in a while I caught her peeking at me with her lovely green eyes. After an hour's delay the train started up again. I gave Megan some space by going to the club car to get us both lunch.

Since she trusted me enough by then not to lock me out, I vowed to make her like me before we reached our stop in Sanford, Florida.

We'd gone from 'fine' to 'nice of you.' Megan didn't know it but I planned to drive her to Crystal River. After all, it was on my way and Mom says I'm a nice guy.

***

After unloading Dad's 1965 Oldsmobile Dynamic 88 and putting the top down, I stashed my duffle on the floor in the back seat and drove to the bus stop where Megan waited for the Orlando to Crystal River bus.

"Hi, need a ride? I'm going right by Crystal River. No waiting." I wiggled my eyebrows Tom Selleck style.

She glanced at the five people — an elderly couple and a couple with a teenager — waiting with her for the bus, then shook her head. "I don't think so."

"Hey, come on. We already spent the night together, the least I can do is drive you home. Toss your bags in the back and hop in."

Megan turned three shades of red, studied the people around her, some of whom giggled, and put her bags in the car.

"This is coercion, you know."

"Yeah, but it got you in the car." I pulled away from the curb to cheering and applause from the crowd.

***

Glad I took the train that day, I think as I set up the car seat/stroller. I tucked the carriage frame, along with the three carry-ons, away in the tiny closet of compartment one twenty-three, leaving the car seat on the train seat, hoping little Jason with his green eyes didn't mind riding backward on the train. You see I not only got Megan to like me, I got her to love me, marry me, and she gave me this little bundle of joy. To celebrate, we're on our way to see Jason's grandparents. He's their Christmas present this year.

Here they come now. This time, there's plenty of room for my wife and son on the Christmas train to Florida.

About the Author

Pat Marinelli, a freelance writer, knows what it's like to be a snowbird but was surprised to discover people actually do wear winter coats or that it can freeze at Christmas time in Florida.

Pat's in-print short stories can be found in the *Snowbird Christmas and Crime Scene: New Jersey* anthologies. She lives in Central Jersey with her husband and two rescue cats, Smoki and Jakette. You can reach Pat on her website at http://www.PatMarinelli.com

Tradition At Cattleman's Junction

Nancy Quatrano

Ellie had towed the hay roll into the pasture for the cattle and forked fresh hay into the stalls for her two Cracker horses, Dale and Roy. She wrapped her arms around Dale's neck and nuzzled the rusty-colored mane.

"I love you, you know," she whispered.

Roy whinnied and nudged her shoulder with his muzzle.

"I love you, too," she laughed.

Exhausted from the endless long days, she relished the rare moments when all the farm work was done and she could enjoy the animals. A coyote cried off in the distance and Dale shied out of her embrace.

"It's okay. The dogs are on duty tonight."

With a stroke of affection for each of the horses she'd owned for over ten years, she closed the barn door tight and dropped the bar into place to keep the doors from opening.

The air was cold for December in northern Florida and she could see her breath. As she walked toward the farmhouse, the timer clicked and the Christmas lights came on, illuminating the small conical-shaped cedar tree she'd decorated in the front yard. Tiny lights of blue, green, red, yellow, and orange wrapped the pillars and railing of the sagging wooden porch. The five-point star shone brightly above the nativity nestled beside the archway that marked the driveway to the Junction Ranch.

"Looks a lot like Christmas to me," she said to the stars above. "Mama, I hope you can see this. I sure miss you and Papa a lot. Happy Anniversary."

Once inside the old house, she put wood into the small stove in the kitchen, stripped out of her filthy jeans and sweatshirt, and climbed the stairs to take a hot shower. She still had cookies to bake and deliver to the church for the children's party on Christmas Eve. It seemed these days like she was never done...

***

Ellie enjoyed the children's laughter and found herself smiling as she watched them scamper around the fellowship hall at the Junction Church. She hoped that Josh would show up in time for refreshments so they could talk a while. He hadn't been by for weeks and she missed his visits. They were both always so busy with their homesteads, they had little time for much else, but he'd said he would be there, so she glanced at the door every now and then. She felt more like a teenager than a woman of twenty-nine.

"Miss Ellie, Miss Ellie," three-year-old Bonnie Sue called to her. "Here is a present for you!"

She dashed across the bare wood floor and nearly collided with Ellie. The small package with a bright red ribbon around it teetered on the fingertips of her tiny outstretched hand.

Surprised, Ellie reached for the box and the little girl, just in time to prevent either one from hitting the floor.

With a giggle, Bonnie Sue dashed away and hid behind her mother.

Where did this come from?

While all eyes were on her, the room suddenly got quiet and she felt her face grow warm. Bells jingled from far away. As everyone stood in silence, the bells grew louder and louder until Ellie heard the unmistakable beat of hooves.

"Whoa!" roared a voice from just outside the hall door. "I said, whoa!" the voice hollered again. "Stop!" shouted the driver in frustration.

Adult laughter rippled around the room while the children stood riveted to the floor like carved wooden soldiers, eyes unblinking as they stared at the door.

In strode a tall, lean man in a red felt suit, complete with a full white beard, a red cap, and shiny black boots. But Ellie knew those twinkling blue eyes. She bit back her smile, the gift clutched in her hands forgotten.

Santa settled his bag of gifts beside the rocking chair that sat in front of the Christmas tree. The children clamored around him like bees to a hive. His laugh was authentic and his joy genuine.

"So, let's all get into a line and then I can talk to each of you," Santa said.

Parents herded children into some sort of order and one by one, each little face stared adoringly into the blue eyes of Santa, whispered something into his ear, and then jumped down from his lap with a wrapped toy clutched in their small hands.

The men drifted away to put the covered dishes on the buffet table so that all could sit down together and have a Christmas meal as soon as Santa was finished with the little ones.

Ellie sat down to watch them as they paraded past her, showing her their new toy fire truck or farm tractor or doll. She made sure to speak to each one and to display utter amazement at the wonderful new gift they possessed.

When the bag was empty and every child was the proud owner of something from Santa, he looked into the bag and frowned. Then he looked at Ellie, who still had the box with the big bow, sitting at her side.

"Where did you get that box, young lady?" Santa asked from his chair.

Bonnie Sue giggled. "I gived it to her, Uncle Santa."

Santa stroked his beard and continued to stare at Ellie. "I see. Santa wanted to give that to Miss Ellie, honey."

Ellie started to feel her face redden as all eyes were upon her and the tall bearded fella. He got to his feet and in three strides he stood before her.

"Where's your big belly, Santa?" she whispered when he leaned down to pull her to her feet.

"That blasted puppy ate it while I was in town today. I'm out of pillows and didn't have time to figure anything else out by the time I got home."

"Kiss her already, Josh!" someone yelled from the kitchen.

"Don't you dare, Josh O'Malley. I'll just die of embarrassment," she hissed at him.

He laughed, then knelt on one knee. The clanking of chairs and plates and knives and forks suddenly ceased and Ellie sucked in a breath. Josh picked up the box with the red bow and handed it to her.

"Christmas is about love and new beginnings and living life for others, Ellie. And I surely love you. Would you do me the honor of becoming my wife?"

Ellie couldn't breathe, or speak, or even see through her tears. Josh's eyes filled with tears, too. "Don't you say no, Ellie Pontier. I'll just die of embarrassment," he whispered.

Ellie undid the bow with trembling fingers and opened the box. She looked at Josh and saw the love in his eyes, the hope in his expression.

"I'd be honored to be your wife, Josh O'Malley. This is the best Christmas present ever!"

The crowd roared and yipped and laughter filled the old grange hall as it had for over two hundred Christmases before.

Just like when Papa proposed to Mama on that Christmas Eve forty years ago.

She wrapped her hand in his, leaned toward him, and kissed his cheek. "You're going to have a tough time beating this next year, Santa."

His blue eyes sparkled with the challenge. "We'll think of something, Ellie Girl, you'll see."

About the Author

Published in short fiction as both Nancy Quatrano and N. L. Quatrano, this author adores mysteries with a bit of happily-ever-after thrown in. She's an instructor, freelance writer and micro-publisher, and owner of On-Target Words, a professional writing business. She can be contacted through www.ontargetwords.com or at nancy@ontargetwords.com.

The Elf Under the Shelf

Mark Reasoner

I was enjoying my usual routine one morning in the week before Christmas. I sat alone in the quiet coffee shop well before sunrise with only two young baristas behind the counter for company. I had my large steaming cup of the house blend, the day's edition of the *Times-Union* open on the table and was peacefully enjoying the calm and stillness when I heard a voice.

"Hey, buddy!"

I looked up to see who'd spoken but didn't see anyone. The baristas were silently brewing coffee. I thought I was imagining things when I heard it again.

"Hey, buddy, down here. Under the shelf."

I looked over to where the creamers, sugar and everything were set out and saw a creature crawl out from underneath. He was about two feet tall, had pointed ears, a hooked nose and wore a tight green costume with a red conical hat.

I looked at my coffee and wondered if the kids had put a *different* kind of shot into it.

"Be cool, man," the creature said. "I'm really an elf."

Uh, yeah — right, I thought. *This is interesting...*

"Okay, you're an elf," I said. "So, don't you belong on the shelf?"

"I belong at the North Pole," he said as he climbed onto the chair across from me. He had to stand on the seat for me to see him.

"Can I get a booster seat for you?" I said as I folded my paper.

"Shut up!" he whined. "I need your help. I missed my ride."

"What do you mean?" I asked, playing along.

"Just what I said," he replied. "I missed the sleigh's takeoff and I need to get where Santa can pick me up."

Yeah, there was definitely something strange in my coffee. Or maybe I wasn't awake yet. I couldn't possibly be having a conversation with a real Christmas elf, could I?

Oh, what the heck, I thought, *let's see where this goes.*

"So why don't you just call him to come back for you?" I asked.

"I tried, but they're over Manitoba about now, and reception is really lousy. I did send a text.

"And I need to get to the airport," he continued, "It's not like you can just land a large sleigh and eight reindeer anywhere."

"Why the airport?" I asked. "Why not just a big parking lot or open space?"

"Why do you think, man?" he said, "We need a place that's secure and isolated. Where better than at an airport? We can be out of the way, and if anyone noticed, it would look like just another landing or takeoff. I mean, can you imagine how people would react if Santa landed out front here?"

He had a point there. I guess Santa would need a place where he could land and take off safely and quietly.

"Why not call a cab," I said. "You've got a phone."

"No money."

"You're kidding me," I said, laughing. "Doesn't Santa pay you guys?"

"Of course he does," he replied, "I just didn't think I'd need any cash. We were supposed to be in and out in an evening."

Hold on a second, I thought. *What was this about being in and out? Christmas Eve was still a few days off.*

"What are you talking about? Santa's not due until the twenty-fourth."

"We came down early for a special celebration at Mayport," he answered, "There are four ships deploying for a year in the Mediterranean. So we brought presents for the crews and their families early. Santa didn't think it was right for them to miss this year."

"Okay," I answered, "so what happened? How'd you get left behind?"

"I was tagging along with some kids on a tour of one of the ships. Lost track of time, and the sleigh was flying away when I finally came topside."

His cell phone chirped and he took it out. I finished my coffee while he read the message and replied. When he finished, he put the phone away and started to climb down from the chair.

"They're on the way," he said. "I have to go now or I won't make the pick-up." He looked at me with wide eyes. "So, please," he went on, "if you can help me out, let's go."

When I didn't move, he continued. "Come on, I can make it worth your while."

"How?" I asked.

"I can see that you don't get coal in your stocking. I'll make sure you're on the nice list, and not the naughty one."

That worked for me. We left the shop. As we walked toward my car, I realized that after an extra brief glance, no one seemed to think it odd that someone two feet tall with pointed ears was walking along the sidewalk beside me. I also realized I didn't know his name. I asked him as I keyed the remote to unlock the doors.

"Murray," he said.

I stopped dead in my tracks.

"What?" he said as he turned to me. "— you think elves always have names like Crumpet or Snowflake or something?"

"Well, I..."

"Oh, good grief," he said. "The old man retired those silly names years ago. Besides, Murray was my grandfather's name."

The drive to Jacksonville International was quiet and uneventful. As we approached the airport proper, Murray told me to turn and take the road around to the back side, toward the Florida Air National Guard hangars.

"So, how does this work?" I asked, "Do you sneak under the fence?"

He gave me an exasperated look.

"No," he said, "just drop me at the guard shack. I can check in there and they'll get me to the runway when the sleigh lands. Simple."

As he got out of the car, I reminded him about making sure I wasn't on Santa's *bad* list. "Hey, Murray," I said, "Can you really make sure I'm on the nice list for Christmas?

"That depends," he said, smiling, "What have you been up to?"

I didn't reply.

"That's okay," he said as he started to walk away. "He already knows."

About the Author

Mark Reasoner is a Hoosier by birth, a teacher by profession and a storyteller by nature. His writings have appeared in *Folio Weekly*, the *DeKalb Literary Arts Journal* and corporate publications. As a software trainer, he develops and narrates computer-based training sessions. He lives and writes in Neptune Beach, Florida.

Unexpected Gifts

C. L. Roman

Sharp fingers of winter air poked at his nose and he scowled. *I can't believe they turned us out,* he thought. *And on Christmas Eve, too.*

Nip stomped over to the rock where his new wife rested and sat down to hold her hand. He didn't regret his decision to marry Pogo against his father's wishes. He had known there would be consequences, but he hadn't realized they would be this severe. He could hear Pogo's teeth chattering through the darkness. Hoping the sound wouldn't carry to the owl hunting overhead, he hugged her close and rubbed her arms.

Around them the forest held its frosted breath. Wan strands of moonlight filtered through the ice lined leaves above the shivering pair. A shadow swooped over them and Nip tensed.

Pogo waited until the shadow passed. "I'm sorry, Nip," she said, her voice as thin and brittle as a thread stitched over snow. "I'll try to be quieter."

He gave her an affectionate squeeze. "As if you could be quieter," he teased, and pulled her to her feet. "You make rabbits sound loud."

She pulled her knit cap tighter over her ear points and tried to smile. "You're right," she said. "It's *you* should watch your noise, as usual."

Nip adjusted his pack straps and pushed his sword into a better angle for walking. The pair trudged across the snowpack, careful to keep a single file so that only one set of tracks showed. Fewest marks made, quickest covered up, his mother had always said. And pixies were so small and light, they usually made no marks at all. But then, they didn't usually travel in winter either.

He grinned. "Me? Hah, I can be as quiet as..."

"Not a mouse, don't say a *mouse*. Although, being that mice are *never* quiet, you may be right. You..."

"Shhh," he stopped her with a finger to his lips. "What's that?"

A reedy scrap of music drifted along the wind and, in the distance, a light glowed golden in the bleak air. She stared at him with round, gray eyes.

"It's not pixies," she said.

He swallowed hard and nodded. "Humans," he said. A speculative gleam lit his gaze and Pogo tugged at his shirt sleeve.

"Nip, no," she said. "You know they can't be trusted."

"Some can't," he agreed, but his voice was far away and his eyes were on the light. "But we needn't show ourselves.

"If there's a cat or a dog, we won't have a choice," she said, but the stern tone was ruined by a shiver and the chattering of her teeth.

"There's little choice betwixt the stone and the stream, love. Shall we be drowned or crushed?" He took her hands and looked into her eyes. "Pogo, there's light and warmth, and I'd wager no owls inside. We'll stay only 'till the ice on our shoes melts and we've thawed a bit."

She shook her head and tightened her jaw. "It's not

safe, it's..."

The screech of a hunting owl split the night and Nip muffled a curse. Taking her hand he ran, pulling her along behind. Pogo flung a frightened glance over her shoulder and uttered a tiny scream of terror. The dark face and wingtips were so close she could see moonlight glinting off its extended talons and the black slash of its gaping beak.

Ahead of them the path dropped into a ravine. Large outcroppings of rock rose on either side, creating a shadowed area where ice had formed. Nip saw the patch of ice and nearly turned his step to avoid it, but then kept running. Beyond the path, the light beckoned. If they could get there in time they would be safe, at least for the moment.

Above them, the owl closed in, angling his wings to check his speed and adjust his descent for the kill.

"Jump and skate!" Nip shouted, and yanked Pogo forward, into the air.

She leapt instinctively, softening her knees to maintain her balance when she landed on the ice. Spraddle-legged, whooping with a fierce, reactive joy, the couple shot over the slick surface, pushing hard to increase their speed. Missing his targets, the owl slammed into the snow behind them, squawking in hungry frustration.

Nip glanced over his shoulder and shouted with laughter at the sight of the indignant bird, but Pogo shushed him. "Not safe yet," she said.

His laughter died as he watched the owl launch himself from the earth. Joining hands, the couple scrambled madly over the wet slush of the well-traveled path.

The owl screeched again and swooped down. Pogo shrieked as her knit cap was lifted from her head and the predator's sharp talons parted her hair.

"Quick — that boulder," Nip panted, and they sprinted across the open ground, skidding to a halt under the scanty shelter offered by a large oval stone jutting over the path edge.

The owl wheeled and screamed after them, fluttering and flapping over the rock. The pixies cowered, pressing themselves into the moss-covered wall at their backs. Nip pushed Pogo behind him and drew the needle sword at his hip. It wouldn't suffice against an enemy this large, but perhaps he could give Pogo time to get away.

Prevented from pouncing on them by the overhang, the owl landed and lunged forward. Nip thrust at the snapping, hooked beak, delivering it a sharp, but ineffectual poke.

"Oh, don't hurt him," Pogo said. "He only wants his dinner."

Nip shot her an incredulous look over his shoulder. "He wants *us* for dinner, you nit."

"Well, I…" her comment ended in scream as the bird attacked again, grabbing Nip's outthrust sword in its beak, and wresting it from his hand. Nip spread his arms and planted his feet.

"When I say go, you run," he said.

"Run where?" she asked, and the owl gave an eerie screech, as if laughing at them.

"Here now, you'll get coal in your stocking if you act that way." The high, booming voice came from overhead and, to Nip and Pogo, it looked as if two small trees had learned to walk. Trees covered in bizarre wool coats patterned with red and white candy-cane stripes, dotted with…no, it couldn't be. Nip rubbed his eyes and stared. Elf faces?

The owl uttered a distinctly undignified squawk and flapped off in a huff.

The trees disappeared, replaced by a giant face, blue-eyed and capped with a riot of blond curls beneath a green knit cap. "Hello," she said. The force of the voice knocked the pixies to the ground and the face puckered with concern. "Oh dear, I'll have to be a bunch more careful than that." A giant hand reached for them. Nip screamed. Pogo fainted.

***

"I'm really sorry I scared you," the giant said, and blew on her cocoa before taking a sip. A fire danced in the stone hearth and Nip was seated on a pixie sized chair with deep cushions and a soft blanket over his knees. Pogo slept nearby under a warm quilt in a pixie sized, elegantly carved bed. It paid to be rescued by a human with a fully furnished doll house.

"Couldn't be helped, Avery" he said. "We are grateful that you showed up when you did. That owl..."

She shook her head. "They don't usually hunt this close to the farm. He only wanted his supper."

Nip snorted. "True, but I'd rather not be his main course." He eyed her curiously. "Are you sure you don't have any pixie blood?"

"Pretty sure," Avery said and laughed. "But it would be fun if I did." She looked around the room. "Isn't it funny? Just this morning, Mom asked if I wanted to give the doll house to the church Christmas auction, but I said no, not this year. And she said I should, 'cause some other kid might could use it since I don't, being twelve and all. But I didn't want to and so we didn't and, well, now you're here." She nodded with youthful wisdom. "Just shows you, some gifts are fated."

Nip looked around him at the dollhouse; a miniature colonial mansion, complete with a portico and Doric columns at the front door. Pogo was sleeping in the master suite. Then he thought about the Jack Russell terrier and the Maine Coon cat asleep on the rug in the human's living room. "We can't stay here forever," he said at last.

Avery sighed and leaned forward. "No, I don't guess you can. But, you'll be safe for the winter at least. And I know a place we can fix up for you by spring, right on the edge of the woods." She leaned back, confident and relaxed. "It'll work out. Mom says if you hold on to hope and trust, something good always comes, especially at Christmas."

He peered at her, eyebrows raised, pointed ears perked. Finally he nodded, "Yes, I had forgotten, but it is true. Christmas gifts have a long habit of showing up in the most unexpected of places."

***

The tall, dry weeds rustled over their heads as they walked through the shrouding dark. A sweet wind blew its frosted breath down their collars, pinning their ear points to their skulls and encouraging cold fingers to take refuge in long, brown sleeves.

"She'd never ask for this," Pogo whispered.

"No," Nip agreed and took his wife's hand. "But she saved us, and now our gift can save her."

Pogo's dark eyes filled and she nodded. "Ok." Then she grinned behind her tears. "Which one will we ask?"

Nip looked around. To their right stood an old, clapboard farmhouse, gray with age, but stalwart still. The yard was studded with trees. A crabbed hawthorn and two lofty pines hunched companionably in the starlit dark, but they were not close enough. In the house's corner window a light glowed, glimmering through the black branches of a leafless oak.

"That one," he said.

"He is very old," Pogo said, with doubt plain in her voice. "Are you sure he will agree?"

"He has watched her grow up. He is watching her die. He will agree."

The pair joined hands and crossed to the ancient sentinel. Nip placed a gentle palm against his trunk and asked, "Will you help us?"

A soft pulse caressed his fingertips. "Yes," the tree rustled and the pixie nodded, satisfied.

Clasping right hands, their left hands green and faintly glowing against the rough bark, the three made the knot. Together they sang.

The air swirled around them with the sudden flurry of snow and ice. The oak shivered and drew in upon himself, as if holding his breath for a long plunge under water, containing his life force so as not to melt the pixie's efforts. White crystals surged from the couple's finger tips. Fantastic traceries of gothic creatures revealed themselves in frosted arabesques, sculpted by song. Faster than thought, the ice raced up the trunk, out over the branches, weaving lace, leaping, dancing out to the tiniest limb and twig until an ice-castle stood before Nip and Pogo — the tree's branches transformed into minarets soaring into the night sky, winking back hope and starlight.

They stood back and Nip put his arm around Pogo's shoulders, cuddling her close as weariness flooded over them.

"Will she see it, Nip? Will she greet the morning?"

He stared at the window through the glistening branches, peering across time as much as space and saw the woman who had been the girl who saved them. His smile was dipped in sorrow, but it survived.

"She will, and more. The ice will guard her through the winter, the melt will keep her through the spring, and then..."

Pogo smiled and a yawn surprised her. Clapping all four fingers of one hand over her lips as her eyes grew wide, she giggled and then stroked his cheek. "Who knows what might happen by summer? It was worth the cost."

He cupped his hand around hers and nodded. "Yes."

Arm in arm they tottered across the winter crusted yard to the home the girl-become-woman had hollowed out for them; hidden away, safe and secure. They were exhausted and older by a year, but content in their bargain. He pushed aside the flat door and the two slipped past the knotted, oval entrance, stepping into warmth. Behind them rose the gift Avery would never ask for, never expect: natural magic made life. He hoped it would be enough.

About the Author

Cheri L. Roman is a writer, editor, teacher, wife, mother, grandmother and friend, in whatever order works best in the moment. Most days you can find her on her blog, The Brass Rag, or working on the next novel in her fantasy series, *Rephaim*. Cheri lives with her husband and two Chihuahuas in Florida. Her website is www.thebrassragcnr.wordpress.com and she loves visitors.

There's a Song in the Air

Drew Sappington

'Twas in the bleak midwinter time...earth lay like iron, and water like a stone.

A brutal breeze blew from off the Atlantic, hammering the wind-chill factor down, down, down. Deep into the seventies.

"Say again 'bout that 'bleak midwinter' thing?" asked Rob.

"It's a Christmas carol," said Jamie. "Well, it's not one of your biggies, but it helps make my point. This is not Christmas weather."

"Whaddya talking about? Just because it's not the way it was *up North* doesn't mean there's something wrong." Rob turned up the collar of his Polo shirt. If the temperature kept plunging, he was going to have to switch from shorts to full-length pants. Bleak midwinter time indeed.

"Look," said Jamie. "I'm not knocking St. Augustine. This is a great place. I even love the weather, most of the time. Except this time of year. Just listen to the songs, the carols. They'll tell you how it's supposed to be —

White Christmas, Winter Wonderland...you need snow to make the season really work."

"I don't know," said Rob. "*White Christmas*?" He pointed at the beach. "You want white? You got white." He swept his arm at the dunes and sea oats, the low waves, the first bright stars hanging in the darkening sky, the last smear of orange to the west. "*Winter Wonderland*? I think we got it."

"*Jingle Bells*. You know, 'one horse open sleigh.' "

"You guys do a lot of sleigh riding in Newark?"

" 'When the snow lay round about, smooth and crisp and even,' " Jamie persisted. "From *Good King Wenceslas*."

"Not sure about the snow part, but with the tide going out that sand's got 'smooth, crisp and even' going for it."

"Look, Wenceslas didn't have that good page fetch pine logs hither just to walk on some beach. You don't get it. There's a whole tradition about the way things are supposed to be. 'Jack Frost nipping at your nose —' "

"Nipping at our feet anyway. Getting where I can't stand to wade for more than a few minutes. Look, Christmas don't have to be white, even going by the songs," Rob pointed out in his slow southern drawl. "You got your green Christmas. That song Bing Crosby sang, *Mele Kalikimaka*, one that goes '*Here we know that Christmas will be green and bright.*' And isn't there one about 'I'll have a blue, blue Christmas?' "

A shooting star streaked across the sky, and they both went, "Whoa."

A star, a star, something something in the night, with a tail as big as a kite.

The stars had colors here in Florida, the planets had size, heft. The Milky Way was thick. It was the kind of night when herald angels might *really* sing, might bend near the earth to touch their harps of gold. Robb and Jamie held their breath, listened to the rippling waves gently sighing against the shore. *Silent night....*

"Come to think of it," Jamie said, "There was another Christmas with palm trees and sand and mild winter breezes."

About the Author

Drew Sappington has worked as a college professor, clinical psychologist and pest control guy. He has published Hidden History of St. Augustine, one textbook, forty articles in professional psychology journals, and a few pieces in outlets that people actually read.

He can be reached via email at drewsappington@msn.com.

Tibetan Horn

Claire Sloan

Cal and I spent our first Christmas together as snow-birds in the Himalayas. We arrived in Thailand at the same time as Joan and Jim Biggerstaff, who were also newlyweds and working at the International School of Bangkok (ISB) where my husband had signed on as principal. Together with other faculty members from ISB, we organized a journey through tiny lands embedded between Tibet and India.

Travel, in my vocabulary, had always meant vacations in Europe enjoying culinary delights, museums, wandering through back alleys, and attempting foreign languages.

Our exotic and stunning Himalayan excursion made for a continual and changing kaleidoscope, a pinch-yourself experience. Sights, smells, clothing, topography, faces — all new, all unfamiliar — yielded a delicious mélange for the senses. We were thrilled with our first stop, Kathmandu, except for having to dodge people hawking and spitting phlegm on the street. (Seasonal colds, I was told.) Our hotel, not significant in amenities or decor, overlooked the majestic peak of Annapurna. Haunted by the spirits of Sir Edmond Hillary and the Sherpas, we walked Katmandu's unpaved streets.

Dinner each night took place at Boris's restaurant, where we usually chose the tasty *mystery* stew. Even if the meal weren't as delicious as it was, Boris was a charming host. He obviously enjoyed eating at his own restaurant. A former ballet dancer, he humorously deprecated himself as a "belly" dancer. Considering his girth, the description was appropriate.

Arriving at our next stop, Bhutan, we learned of a monastery, invisible through the clouds. We immediately hired a guide to take us to what seemed to be a nearby peak. It was close, but only as the crow flew. The following morning, our group left the hotel only to embark upon the most terrifying bus ride I've ever experienced. The narrow road we descended was poorly maintained and had no guardrails. We left our small plateau, swooped far down the winding road, and after what seemed to be forever, we climbed another pinnacle, gaping down on serpentine cliffs from the top of the world.

The spectacular views were pure terror for me, and each time I opened my eyes to see if we were there yet, I saw only the flimsiest ribbon of road ahead. It was as though the bus were balanced on a tightrope.

When our small group eventually arrived, white-knuckled but intact, we congratulated each other on being alive. I wanted to decompress, but that need passed once I'd entered through the monastery's massive doors. Wordless, our group gravitated together, struck speechless with awe.

Throughout the temple's immense central room, monks of all ages, in deep red-orange robes, reclined on the floor, chanting and supporting or blowing immense Tibetan horns equal to their stature. Their instruments were copper with decorative white-metal trim. The five-foot horns played in unison, transforming the atmosphere with their melodic bass sounds, ethereal, yet mesmerizing.

The enlarged "collector" gene in my DNA, instantly instructed me to possess my own horn. However, it wasn't as if I could take Macy's elevator to the Tibetan Horn department and pay with my American Express card. The Internet didn't even exist then, nor had e-Bay been spawned. Our absentee guide conveniently reappeared once negotiations had been concluded and informed us of a gift shop no one had even noticed near the monastery entrance. We probably overlooked it in our frightened state upon arrival.

When the concert of music and chanting ceased, the guide subtly informed us that the gawking phase was over and it was time to leave. We gratefully thanked the monk who had welcomed us in and placed a substantial offering in a nearby bowl. To our amazement, he barred our exit in the universal language of outstretched arms. My eyes fled to the massive doors that were linked with equally significant bolts. First, I thought it was a joke. Then I thought it was a misunderstanding. Wrong on both counts.

Most of us had brought enough cash for an offering and tips for the driver and guide. One person negotiated with the monk in charge, and the rest pooled extra resources, making up for those who didn't anticipate a need for ransom. After much haggling, one ante brought a smile to the monk in charge, and we were finally allowed to pass through the same portals we entered.

Once outside in the bright sun and crisp air, there was a sprinkling of nervous laughter. Magically, or so it seemed, doors opened to a small kiosk, and there was the gift shop about which I had, by then, forgotten. We made a quick perusal of the merchandise and exited minutes later, a few of us carrying Buddhist horns. Oddly enough, we could fit these huge instruments on the bus and subsequently on the plane to Bangkok, because they collapsed into a size no longer than two feet.

The following Christmas, as a result of plane schedules and school holiday dates, we didn't leave Bangkok for the winter break until after Dec 25th. By then, Bangkok was our home, less surprising, less mysterious than when we arrived. Without the exotic distraction of something new, we ex-pats became more conscious of missing stateside friends and families, missing the cold, the snow, and the trappings of the season — especially the evergreen tree with its tinsel and the ubiquitous gifts placed beneath.

Although Bangkok was one abundant department store for tourists, it had not yet prepared for the sale of live trees. Neither pine nor spruce nor anything similar was available for hundreds of miles. (Only years later did fake trees become prevalent.)

I missed my daughter Hillary, who was at college in the US, and if wine hadn't been outrageously expensive in Thailand, I might have used it to drown my homesickness. I felt somewhat assuaged when the Biggerstaffs invited some friends to Christmas dinner. Leaving our shoes at their door, Thai style, we treaded barefoot across polished floors of teak parquet.

We had no expectations of traditional ham, turkey, or goose, but thoughts of food vanished at the sight of the most unique Christmas tree I'd ever witnessed. There, in the corner of the immense living room, was a copper Buddhist horn, shiny, stately, and elegant. On top was an origami paper star, sprinkled with silver dust. Twisted green ribbon streamers fastened beneath the star fanned out beyond the wider base of the horn in an inverted cone shape — a stylized Christmas tree. Joan's resolve to fashion a symbolic tree and her clever rendition were more than an expression of artistry. It spoke of her determination to problem-solve until she found a unique solution.

For years, even after returning to the States, I carried

on the tradition. My good friend is gone, but my Tibetan horn reminds me of her, her lessons to persevere, and a very special Christmas in a very special land.

About the Author

Claire is a world traveler and a true believer in the magic within all human beings. A teacher by profession, a gifted writer, and a woman of grace and good taste, she is seeking representation for her YA novel titled, *Then You Can See the Sky* and completing the work on a compelling Civil War novel.

She is a member of the Florida Writers Association and resides in St. Augustine Beach, Florida. Claire can be contacted by email at cmsloan3@yahoo.com.

The Christmas Goose

Skye Taylor

Jeff was late. Resentment, despair, and anger over-
came my limited patience. I couldn't take the holiday
music and festive decorations a moment longer. Not
when I was facing the worst Christmas of my life.

I worked my way past a crowd of carolers just coming through the door. Fresh air felt good on my face and
in my hair in spite of the dismal gray chill. The sudden
quiet, broken only by distant traffic, suited my mood. I
felt alone and cut off from everything I had once been.
All I really wanted was Julie.

Except, I'd said goodbye to Julie.

Not *goodbye, see you tomorrow,* but *goodbye, and
have a nice life.*

I jerked my chair onto the path we had traveled so
many times during rehab. Me helpless in the chair. Julie
pushing.

Julie had been at my bedside when I finally regained
consciousness. I don't recall what I said to her, but it
must have been pretty strange because she'd cracked up.
I'd been in a drug-induced fog and hadn't seen the tears

mixed into her laughter.

She'd missed a whole semester of college to be at my side. But it was time to set her free. She didn't need an anchor for the rest of her life. Julie loved to dance. I didn't have legs to dance on. She dreamed of traveling to far-away places. I had trouble just making my way to the mailbox. Julie wanted kids. What if I could no longer give her even that? Julie deserved better than me.

Julie disagreed, but she hadn't seen me struggling in rehab. She hadn't seen me throw my specially-made prosthesis at the wall in frustrated anger. She hadn't heard me screaming in pain. Or waking from a nightmare. She'd be better off if she never did.

My chair lurched to a stop when it left the paved path. I cursed and wrestled it forward. I hated my new reality. I'd been a track star in high school, excelling in high jump and hurdles. Now I'd never jump again and just getting out of bed was a hurdle.

Sweating and still cursing, I finally got myself down to the pond. When I'd asked Julie to bring me here three days ago, the sparkle in her eyes had told me she expected me to propose. Instead, I'd told her to take a hike.

All I'd ever considered being when I grew up was a cop. But in our family, military service came first. What kind of run-down police force hires a cripple? I had no idea how I was going to support myself for the next fifty years, never mind a wife and kids.

No reasons left to endure the desert my life had become. Julie had taken my heart with her, along with the sun and laughter and everything that had made the last few months bearable.

I didn't see the goose until my wheels crunched into a pile of dead leaves, and made her flinch. She eyed me with alarm and tried to move away, but a broken wing made escape impossible. We gazed at each other in shared misery. Then her attention turned elsewhere.

A gander glided gracefully in and landed between us.

They should have flown south months ago, but clearly her injury had kept them grounded. Somewhere I'd read that geese mated for life. The faithful male made soft sounds in his throat while his mate ate the food he'd brought her. Apparently deciding I was no threat, he took a couple running steps and soared back into the air. A few minutes later he returned with another offering.

Did the gander know his mate would probably never fly again? Perhaps instinct told him she wouldn't, but it hadn't mattered. She was his mate and if she couldn't go, then neither would he.

My eyes stung. Julie had shown me the same kind of faithfulness, but I had turned her away. I'd convinced myself it was for her good. I back-handed tears that escaped down my cheeks. I'd been so busy thinking of what I wanted and couldn't have that I hadn't listened to anything she said. Hadn't considered what she wanted that I *could* still give her.

The gander returned once again. He folded his wings and settled in beside his mate. The two sat peacefully in the chilly December air, content in each other's company.

I'd been so wrong. Julie and I shared something special. It had survived the crazy tumult of our teenage years. It had weathered the separation of Boot Camp and college. It had been strong enough to bring her rushing to my bedside the moment the Army had deposited me at Walter Reed. Maybe she hadn't seen the worst of my temper, but she hadn't flinched at the sight of my stumps.

The love I felt for that smart, funny, generous woman had been the center of my universe for almost half my life. We were meant to be life mates. Just like this gander and his goose.

I wiped my palms on my jeans, then gripped the wheels with determination. Maybe it wasn't too late to admit what a jerk I'd been and fix what I'd broken.

***

Jeff pulled up in front of Julie's parent's home. I'd picked her up here a thousand times and seen her run eagerly down the stairs to meet me. Now I prayed she'd even agree to see me. After the things I'd told her three days ago, I wouldn't blame her if she sent her father to the door to send me packing.

Christmas candles winked in the windows and a wreath hung at the door. Then I noticed the newly built ramp. Raw, pressure-treated wood. A handrail at the appropriate height installed with the expectation that I'd be coming often and would want to manage on my own. Shame welled up in me.

Even Julie's parents had accepted who I was now and had made adjustments. They could have wanted so much more for their only daughter.

Jeff opened the car door and unfolded my chair. I waved him away as I shifted myself from the car to the chair. If the Thomas family still had faith in me, then I damned well wasn't going to disappoint them.

Jeff squeezed my shoulder. "I'll text before I leave to make sure you're set."

"Thanks." I set the chair in motion.

As I neared the top of the ramp Julie's dad appeared at the door. He held it open for me. "It's about time you came to your senses, young man."

"Yes, sir," I agreed, pushing myself across the threshold.

Julie stood halfway down the staircase to the upper floor biting her lip. Her eyes looked puffy and raw. My heart contracted with guilt and the sudden fear at what her hesitation might mean.

Christmas music filtered in from the front room. *I'll be Home for Christmas* was playing, and I realized I *was* home. I'd finally come home to the only woman who could ever make my life feel whole again.

I was crying again, but I didn't care. "I'm sorry," I croaked. "I was wrong."

Julie flew into motion, running down the remaining steps. She dropped to her knees and flung her arms about my neck. I heard the door to the kitchen close softly as her father left us alone.

I hugged her close for a long time, then gently pushed her away. I dug in my jacket pocket for the ring Jeff had obligingly stopped at the jewelers for.

"I'd get down on my knees, but I'm afraid I might not be able to get back up," I began lamely.

"Yes!" she shouted before I even had a chance to pop the question. "Yes, yes, yes! This is the best Christmas of my whole life. I love you so much." Her voice rose on the last word as tears spilled out of her beautiful brown eyes.

My hand shook as I pushed the ring onto her finger. It was turning out to be the best Christmas of my life, too. Barely registering the pain, I pulled her onto my lap and kissed her. I poured everything I was feeling into it, hoping she would know how very much I loved her, because I didn't trust my voice at all.

***

I don't know how Julie's mom pulled it together, but eight days later, on Christmas Eve, surrounded by our families and friends and a zillion flickering candles, Julie became my wife. My soul-mate, my friend, my lover for as long as we both shall live. As we sat together in Julie's living room, holding hands and accepting congratulations, I spied a new ornament on her tree. Two gray geese, their necks forming a heart with a holiday wreath encircling them both.

I pulled her closer. "Merry Christmas, little goose," I whispered into her ear. "Merry Christmas forever."

About the Author

Skye Taylor lives on the beach in St. Augustine Florida where she spends her time writing and volunteering at the living history museum in our nation's oldest city. Besides raising four terrific kids, her adventures include two years in the Peace Corps, skydiving and travel to far-away places. She's a member of Romance Writers of America., Ancient City Romance Authors and Florida Writers Association. Her intrigue novel, *Whatever it Takes,* was published in 2012 and she kicked off 2013 with a three book contract from Belle Books for her latest romance series.

Wanda

Elaine Cagneri

It's still dark on Christmas morning, but I whisper to my sisters, "Can we get up yet?"

"Not yet," my older sister Sue replies. "We have to wait until six-thirty."

She's nine and bossy, but she has two years more experience at Christmas mornings, so I bounce my feet against the mattress until the clock's hands move to the magic time.

I'm first as we dash into my parent's bedroom and jump on the bed. "Can we see what Santa brought?" I ask.

"Please," Sue adds.

My father yawns and groans. "So early?" he asks, but starts looking for his slippers. "Let me turn on the lights. Be careful on the stairs."

I hurry after him, but Sue still beats me down. We each have a spot under the tree filled with presents. She's already kneeling on the right over her gifts, opening packages from the ends, folding the wrapping paper into neat strips. On the left, my mother sits with my younger sister Crystal to help her.

My spot is in the middle and has a tall box wrapped in red with green ribbon. It stands about half my size. What could it be? I've asked Santa for more dolls. I love dolls. But this is too big to be a doll. Has he left me some boy's Erector Set? My heart stutters and then pounds. I hope Santa doesn't make mistakes.

I tear into the wrapping and feel my mother watching me. I wonder if she's angry because I'm ripping all the paper and making a mess, but she's smiling. I keep tearing. The monstrous box contains the most beautiful doll in the world. The sash over her blue dress says in large letters that her name is "Wanda." She has long blonde, baloney curls, blue eyes, and pale skin with blushed cheeks. She stands eighteen inches tall. And she can walk. Tiny rollers are molded into the bottoms of her white shoes.

"How do you make her walk?" I ask.

Sue runs over and grabs the key. "I'll do it."

"No, let Elaine do it," my mother says. "You have to wind her up."

"You put the key in here," Sue tells me, inserts the key, and stands back.

I turn the key a couple of times and when I stop, Wanda extends a leg and swings an arm. She does it over and over again and she's walking with a mechanical whir across the living room's hardwood floor. Everyone has stopped opening gifts to watch her, entranced. When her walk ends, I run and hug her. "You are the best dolly in the whole world."

I don't allow myself to be parted from Wanda for the rest of the day. As I eat, she stands watching from the corner of the kitchen. When my grandparents come over, I wind her up and have her walk to Grandma.

"She's perfect," Grandma says, a twinkle in her eye. "Love that blue dress."

Grandpa adds, "Don't wind her too tight or she'll break."

I'll still love her if she breaks. Walking is just a bonus. What I like most about her is her size. She's so big she seems real. I carry her to the porch and tell her stories.

At bedtime, I want to sleep with my doll, so my mother carries her upstairs. Wanda's body is stiff and takes up too much of the bed, but I settle next to her, one arm holding her close. I fall asleep, breathing in her plastic scent.

The next morning, I wake early and dress myself in play clothes. I tuck my doll under my arm and make my way to the stairs. Looking past Wanda's big head, I can't see the step and miss it. She falls with me and I hang onto her, instead of grasping for the banister. My cheek bangs a step. White ceiling and oak whirl by as I roll in a bungled somersault, smashing down the thirteen slippery steps. I land in a heap with Wanda on top of me. Everything is spinning and I'm crying.

My mother bounds down the stairs and pries Wanda from my arms. "Are you hurt?" she asks.

"Is Wanda okay?" I ask before the pain kicks in. "My eye!" I press my hand to it and black out.

I don't remember the trip to the hospital or back home. When I wake up, I'm on the sofa with a cold compress covering my forehead, eye, and cheek. My mother said the doctor thinks I have a concussion and my first black eye. I'm not sure how that will look, one hazel and one black. I hope it doesn't stay that way. He said I can't watch TV for a week, and I have to lie down and rest a lot. That's okay. I don't feel like moving much.

Mom's in the kitchen. I hear her opening a can and butter sizzling in a pan. She's making tomato soup and grilled cheese for lunch. She's told Sue to carry my doll up and down the stairs for me, so having a big sister finally comes in handy.

Wanda survived the fall without injury. She's lying next to me and I have my arm around her. The compress relieves the ache in my head. With my eyes closed, I suck in a large breath of Wanda's satisfying plastic smell. This is still the best Christmas ever.

About the Author

Elaine Togneri is published in fiction, non-fiction, and poetry. Her stories have appeared in Chicken Soup for the Soul anthologies, Woman's World Magazine, and the 2011 MWA Anthology, The Rich and The Dead. Most recently, Plan B Magazine published her short mystery "Shadows." Elaine no longer has her doll Wanda, but cherishes the memories. Visit her website at sites.google.com/site/elainetogneri

The Best Christmas Gift

Judy Weber

Emily jerked, dropping the pot when she heard her daughter's shrieks. Disregarding the mess of string beans scattered around the floor, she headed for the kitchen door, her heart in her throat.

"Amanda, what's wrong?"

She knew as soon as she got outside. Six year old Amanda was holding the dog's leash, but there was no dog attached at the other end. Instead, a body was lying at the edge of the road, its rear end canted at an unusual angle. And Amanda was still shrieking.

Emily was never sure how to deal with Amanda's autism when circumstances changed quickly. The child wasn't able to deal with it, and while she seldom talked, she was undoubtedly able to make lots of noise. And this noise meant she had probably seen Molly get hit.

Emily grabbed the shaking girl, turned her to shield her from the sight of the dog, and ran to a neighbor. "Mrs. Grandy, can you watch Amanda for a while? I've got to get Molly to the vet while she's still alive."

"I saw what happened, Emily. It wasn't Amanda's

fault. That little dog must've heard something and tugged at his collar so hard he pulled right out of it. Leave Amanda with me. I've baked some Christmas cookies, and I need someone to test them — make sure they're okay."

Amanda's autism had been diagnosed shortly after her second birthday, when she was subjected to a battery of tests because she hadn't yet begun to talk. Emily and Tom learned quickly that anything out of the ordinary in Amanda's surroundings produced unexpected reactions. Sometimes it was repetitive movements that neither parent was able to stop; sometimes it was the wailing or keening sound that broke their hearts. They had no other children for Amanda to interact with, and the family doctor said she might not have anything to do with siblings anyway. The child lived in her own world.

They were hesitant to have a pet of any kind, but when they considered getting a dog, they decided to bring Amanda along and see if she would take part in the selection. The yaps of all the dogs should have been upsetting to the girl, but she smiled as she went over to a cage where a cute brown, black, and white puppy wagged furiously at Amanda. She pointed to the dog and said "Molly."

Well, it was lucky that the dog was a female, since it was almost impossible to get Amanda to change her mind after she'd decided on something. The store clerk said, "That dog's part beagle. They make really good pets."

So they took Molly home and soon Emily and Tom found their daughter talking to the dog, when she wouldn't talk to *any* humans. And her smile became automatic when Molly licked her face with a tiny pink tongue. They became almost inseparable.

Emily swiped at her tears. The day was warm, as only a South Florida December morning could be when she drove one-handed to the vet's office, the other holding little blanket-wrapped Molly on her lap. The dog occasionally made a pitiful cry.

When she arrived at the office, she carried the injured dog into the vet's examining room and laid her gently on the table.

"This looks pretty bad, Mrs. Newsome," the old man said. "I can give her something for the pain, but I suggest you put her to sleep."

"I can't do that doctor. It would destroy my daughter. She's autistic and her world right now revolves around that dog. She is closer to that animal than to either my husband or me. Can you operate on her? I don't care what it costs."

"I'll do what I can. I'll operate today and I should know something by tomorrow."

Emily cried as she drove home. Would Christmas be totally ruined? It was a difficult holiday anyway because of Amanda. They couldn't have a big, real tree because its size and sudden appearance in the house upset her. The few decorations inside the house were all small, and there was just a wreath on the front door. Christmas was just three days away. What would they do if Molly didn't make it?

When she retrieved Amanda from Mrs. Grandy's, the child was silent. Emily wasn't able to draw her into conversation at all, not totally unusual. The girl didn't say a word the rest of the day and the silent house that evening reflected Emily and Tom's fears.

The next day, Amanda still didn't speak, and Emily tried to create some normalcy by baking Christmas cookies. She jumped when the phone rang.

"Well, your daughter must live on the side of the angels," the old vet told her. "Molly had no internal injuries, just a couple of broken bones. I've patched up her hip and hind leg. She'll have a cast on that leg for some time, and later on she'll undoubtedly have a limp. But that's still pretty lucky, if you ask me."

"God bless you, doctor. When can we pick her up?"

"Later today. I'm glad you can get her home by Christmas."

Emily took Amanda with her to the veterinarian's office. When they entered the examining room, they found Molly lying on a blanket, her hind leg and hip in a cast. Spotting Amanda, the little dog began to wag her tail.

"Molly, I love you," said Amanda, her first words in two days. She kissed the dog on top of the head, and Molly reached up and licked her face.

Emily put one hand on her daughter's shoulder and the other on Molly's head.

"Thank you, God. This is the best Christmas gift ever."

About the Author

Judy Weber is a writer of murder mystery novels and short stories. After a career as a real estate agent, it was natural for her to create a realtor protagonist who has a penchant for discovering dead bodies. Judy's short stories are generally more heart-warming, or heart-wrenching.

She is a member of the Mystery Writers of America, Sister-in-Crime, and the Florida Writers Association, whose annual anthology will again include one of her short stories. She can be reached at jweber1026@comcast.net.

A Florida Christmas

Sharon Buck

It was a hot and humid seventy-four degrees outside. Of course, this was standard Christmas weather in Florida. Inside the hospital, where everything was climate-controlled by some unseen mega-corporation located in the heartland of America, it was cool on some floors and downright hot on others. I guess it depended on what you were in for.

Getting the call that my attendance was required for the pending apparent departure of my father was not high on my list of things I wanted to do at Christmas time.

While I loved my dad, I didn't particularly like him. Some family members said we were just alike. I didn't see it and rebuked that in the name of Jesus.

I can't honestly say we had a love-hate relationship. It was more like oil and water, we just didn't mix well together. We butted heads constantly when we were together.

After spending god knows how much money ($17,001 to be precise) over the years with various psychologists and talk therapists, I had come to the conclusion there wasn't much difference between them and attorneys. They both will just keep going until they figure out you have no more money to spend and then miraculously decide you are cured, healed, or whatever the current psycho-babble buzzword is for no mo' money.

After much self-analysis, I finally had the epiphany that perhaps I was trying to punish my dad for the humiliation I suffered in seventh grade when he chaperoned the first real boy-girl party I had been invited to.

I didn't know he was going to chaperone until we got to the party and he went in with me. That was embarrassing enough because I saw my friends snickering at me but when he went outside and "patrolled the grounds to make sure none of you kids are getting into any trouble" that's when everyone turned on me. Everyone wanted to have that first kiss and he was taking away the first rites of adulthood. He was stopping adolescence hormonal urges. Hell, that was un-American!

He refused to leave. I begged, I pleaded, I groveled. I told him he was making my life a living hell. He didn't care.

I screamed, "I hate you." The man just laughed at me while I had tears pouring down my face.

Back at school on Monday, that's when the real humiliation began. It was bad enough he was teaching at the same junior high school, it was bad enough that I already had some of his students threatening to beat me up in the girls bathroom on a weekly basis, but the pain of rejection and humiliation escalated to a whole new level with my friends making fun of me for "bringing my daddy" to the party. Even kids who had not been invited to the party taunted me with "where's your daddy?" every opportunity they got.

I was never invited to another boy-girl party the rest of my junior and high school years.

It's amazing what memories come up when confronted with the impending demise of a parent. I had plenty of good memories with him but they just weren't the first things that came to mind. Sad.

Taking a deep breath and letting it out slowly, I had already promised myself I wasn't going to argue with him and I wasn't going to cry. After having a total hysterectomy in my forties, I could control the anger that would occasionally burble to the top but tears, ah, yes, the tears, I couldn't stop them at all. Mad, happy, sad, whatever, the tears could flow at the drop of a hat. I hated feeling like I was out of control. Tears reminded me I had feelings. I was tough, I didn't *need* no stinking feelings!

Even though my sisters had warned me how frail he looked, I wasn't prepared to see his little body looking so small in a hospital bed. And, let's face it, hospital beds aren't known for being large. He wasn't tall by any stretch of the imagination, only a quarter of an inch taller than me, but he only looked to be about three feet tall in the bed.

"Hey, Daddy, how ya feeling?" I leaned over to kiss him.

He wiggled his fingers. Yeah, he's dismissing me again, I thought. That's what he did when he couldn't be bothered or didn't want to answer questions; wiggled his fingers or waggled his hand. Immediately that thought was replaced with love and compassion. A warm flowing of love from the top of my head spread rapidly through my entire body.

His lips were moving but I couldn't hear anything. I leaned closer to hear him, literally almost hovering over his mouth, holding his hand.

"I'm sorry I wasn't a better daddy to you," he whispered.

"You were fine. We've been through this before."

"I never understood you. I'm sorry."

The words caught me totally off-guard. I wasn't expecting that. I looked at him. His eyes were still shut.

"Do what?" I squeaked.

"I never understood you. I wanted a boy but you came instead and I was beyond happy."

"Yeah, well, you never said that. You just always said you wanted a boy." My heart was hard. I didn't want to feel my feelings. I'd spent a lifetime covering them up. I was a master at it.

"I didn't know what to do with you." He paused for a moment and then continued, "I love, loved you, though."

"You had a funny way of showing it by being so critical of everything I said or did. You were hard on me." The bitterness and resentment that I thought had disappeared with all those years of expensive therapy came rushing back. I wanted him to feel the pain he had caused me. I knew it was unfair, he was old, dying, and trying to make peace with me, but I didn't care. My heart was concrete hard.

"I wanted you to be the best, at the top of everything."

"You only wanted it because it made you look good. You didn't care that I didn't want the same things you did. I didn't care about making straight A's. I wanted to have fun and enjoy school. If I made a B+ in something that was really hard for me, it was never freaking good enough for you."

I mimicked him, "Why didn't you make an A? Why didn't you study harder? Why didn't you whatever?" I took a deep breath and continued.

"You created the feeling that I was never good enough or whatever I did, it just was never freaking good enough.

"Dammit, Daddy, why couldn't you *ever* be happy with what I did? I tried my hardest for years to make you happy, make you proud of me but it was never good enough. Whatever I did, it just was never good enough. You were always comparing me to your friends' kids and what they were doing or comparing me to my sisters and their lives. What the hell was wrong with what I was doing?"

By this time I had gotten loud and was mad at myself for hollering at an old man who could not change the past. The little child inside of me let out years of pain, anger, resentment, and frustration not only at him but at myself for trying to please someone who did not have the capacity to return love the way I needed it.

The Greatest Generation, the World War II vets, did not know how to express their feelings. I had spent years and thousands of dollars getting in touch with my feelings...except when it came to my dad, the only real feelings I could express were the anger and the hurt I felt he had caused me.

It suddenly occurred to me that I was acting like a victim, that I wasn't taking responsibility for my own actions and feelings. I felt totally spent, drained. This really wasn't what I wanted him to take to heaven with him, one last fight.

Blinking back tears, I reached for his hand. "I'm sorry, Daddy. I just always tried so hard and it just never seemed like it was good enough for you. That's really my ownership. You did fine."

No answer. No answer for a couple of minutes. I looked to make sure he was still breathing, watched his chest move up and down.

"Daddy, are you still here?" I spoke in a soft voice as tears began to roll down my face. "I love you. I just don't how to make you love me."

"You've got spunk, you're an adventurer, and you'll stand up for what you think is right. I've always admired that about you."

I looked at him, not sure I heard right.

"You've done things I only dreamed about. Things I wish I'd had enough nerve to do. You don't seem to be afraid of anything. I don't understand that and it makes me afraid for you."

He paused. "It makes me proud of you. I *am* proud of you, darling."

I was shocked and tears rolled freely down my face. I didn't know what to say or even what to feel.

"Your job wasn't to make *me* happy; it was to make *yourself* happy. I love you and am proud of you." He opened his eyes slightly, "I just didn't know to tell you that. I'm sorry."

A slight smile tugged at my mouth.

"You were always so much fun as a little girl. I just didn't appreciate your wild enthusiasm for life and new adventures. That's just who you are."

I had turned into a weeping middle-aged woman whose hard heart was broken. I wondered vaguely why breakthroughs often occurred during life and death situations. The little child in me loved her daddy and didn't want him to go.

"Daddy, I love you too. Don't die, Daddy, don't die. I love you," I sobbed uncontrollably. *Damn hormones.*

"It's not my time to go, baby." He opened his eyes and smiled. "Your sisters want to put me in a nursing home. Take me home with you, okay? Please?"

I exploded with so many emotions I had no idea what to do with any of them.

"You want to go to Orlando?" I was shocked and not really prepared to take him back to my home. "Ah, do you really think that's a good idea? I mean, our past and all."

I wasn't sure that this wasn't a temporary reprieve from our constant butting of heads, although, honestly, I knew something had changed deep inside of me...maybe him too.

"No, my house, you can work from there."

Well, that was true. Since all of my work was on the computer and internet, I could do it anywhere.

"Yep, you take better care of me than your sisters do. They don't understand what's happening, not really. I don't think they really want to know."

"Daddy, are you sure about this?"

He nodded his head.

I cradled his head in my arms, kissed him on the head, and said, "Let me go see if I can spring you out of here."

Three hours later, I was wheeling him out of the hospital into the warm, humid weather to take him home. His color had returned, he seemed more energized; he was looking forward to going back to his home.

Suffice it to say, my sisters weren't happy about it, which they expressed quite forcibly, but they weren't willing to change their lives to take him home with them, either.

As I rolled him out to the car, he said, "It's a beautiful Florida Christmas. Thank you and I love you, darling."

He was smiling...and so was I.

About the Author

Sharon Buck is a speaker, senior book marketing consultant and an author coaching other authors to create a national platform to ignite their book sales. She has had five books published and is currently at work on her first fiction novel. Her websites are www.BookAuthorsTour.com and www.OffTheShelvesFast.com. Her email address is Sharon@BookAuthorsTour.com.

A Wing and a Sleigh

Mark Reasoner

"Cool," the young man next to me said.

I looked over and saw the final scene of the classic *Twilight Zone* episode where William Shatner sees a gremlin out on the wing of his plane.

"A classic," I said as I bookmarked and closed the novel I was reading.

"I'm glad I won't have a window seat," he went on. "Seeing that would send me over the edge. Don't know what I'd do if I thought someone was out there trying to bring down the plane."

"Or even just hitching a ride," I said.

"Yeah," he said. "Good thing it can't really happen."

"Well, certainly not tonight," I replied.

"Huh?"

"It's Christmas Eve," I said. "If anyone was hitching a ride on a plane's wing tonight it'd be Santa — not that gruesome thing."

The young man looked at me as if I'd spoken in some unknown language.

Along with a few hundred others, we were sitting in the open gate area at the end of Hartsfield-Jackson

Airport's A concourse. Being Christmastime, the crowds were bigger and flight delays more common. Nothing outlandish, but enough to inconvenience some passengers and a few folks were more irritated than usual. The delays also meant waiting areas were quite crowded and seating at a premium.

I was one of those delayed, with my flight running about an hour late. The young man was waiting for a seat on the flight set to board through one of the other gates in the area. Both of us were killing time as best we could.

Having started down this path, I decided to continue rather than return to my reading.

"Seriously," I said to him, "Don't you think it'd be more appropriate for Santa to hitch the ride tonight?"

"Oh, come on, man," the youngster replied turning to face me, "that old show's a great story, but it's just that. It's not real, and neither is Santa."

"Are you sure about that?" I asked.

"Do I look like I'm seven?" he answered.

"No, but you can still believe in Santa. Work with me —it's Christmas."

He didn't say anything, but didn't turn away either.

"Just think about it for a second," I said, "Say you were looking out there, like the Shatner character, and saw Santa Claus riding on the wing tonight. How would you react?"

Before he could answer, another voice joined the conversation.

"Scotty, get us out of here," it said in a dead-on Captain Kirk impression.

We both turned and looked at the portly gentleman with white hair and beard sitting in the row behind us.

"Sorry," the man said in a joyous baritone. "I couldn't resist."

With three people now involved, we made introductions before carrying on. My seat-mate's name was Brad and the old guy called himself Nick.

"Okay," I said. "Back to the question. How would you react?"

Brad paused for a couple of seconds and then replied, "I'd probably think I was dreaming or hallucinating. Either way, it's nuts."

"You mean you wouldn't ask why?" I said.

Brad didn't answer.

"Think about it," I went on, "here's a guy who goes around the world on Christmas Eve with his own flying transport, able to go anywhere, any time, so why in the world would he need to hook on to the wing of Boeing 757?"

I could see I'd started Brad thinking. While he noodled on this, I turned to Nick and asked him the same question.

"Well," the old man said, "perhaps the sleigh breaks down and Santa has to keep going while it's being repaired."

"That wouldn't work," Brad said.

"Why not?"

"What would he do with the reindeer?" Brad replied. Apparently he'd decided to go along with the concept. "And besides, wouldn't he have a back-up?"

Old Nick chuckled out loud. "Good point young man. He *would* have a back-up."

"Okay," I said, smiling. "It wouldn't be the sleigh. Maybe it's the reindeer. Maybe one of them gets sick or hurt, or they just need a break."

"But wouldn't Santa stay with them?" Nick asked.

"Yeah," Brad said. "And what about his toy sack? How would he keep that with him?"

They had me. I'd started this line of questioning and my two cohorts had boxed me in quite nicely. Even if it was Christmas Eve, any stowaway on our plane's wing would likely not be a jolly old elf.

"Oh well," I said, opening my book, "I guess you're

right. It doesn't work."

"Besides," Brad said, "it's all imaginary. Nothing's going to ride on the wing."

We went back to our reading and were silent for several minutes. Around us, people boarded their flights and the gate area became less populated. Brad's flight began to board and he started gathering his things when his name was called from the stand-by list. Before he could finish packing up, he stopped and turned to us with a smile.

"I got it," he said. "We were right. Santa wouldn't ride a wing, but what about an elf?"

"Why would an elf need to ride on the wing?" I asked.

"To catch up with the old boy. Maybe a present was left behind or a toy got finished late."

Nick and I laughed and clapped our young companion on his back as he moved toward the boarding door.

"Well done, my friend," Nick said, "well done. And Merry Christmas to you."

"Merry Christmas," Brad replied as he headed to the jet way.

As Old Nick and I returned to our seats, I asked one last question.

"What do you really think; would Santa Claus hitch a ride on a plane's wing tonight?"

"No," Nick replied. "He'd buy a ticket and sit inside with everyone else."

"How do you know?" I asked.

"Ho, Ho, Ho," he answered and placed a finger at the side of his nose. "I've found it awfully cold out there at thirty-five thousand feet."

About the Author

Mark Reasoner is a Hoosier by birth, a teacher by profession and a storyteller by nature. His writings have appeared in Folio Weekly, the DeKalb Literary Arts Journal and corporate publications. As a software trainer, he develops and narrates computer-based training sessions. He lives and writes in Neptune Beach, Florida.

Special Holiday Dedication

Ryan's Poem

Wilma Shulman

Author's Note: I wrote this poem as a favor for a friend whose 8-year-old son Ryan had told her he'd decided he no longer believed in Santa Claus.

Hello Ryan,

I'd like to introduce myself by writing this, because
I'm Katarina Kringle—I am *Mrs.* Santa Claus.
Kris Kringle is another name for Santa, and what's
       more
The children of the world gave him a dozen names
       before.
I've looked at Santa's list, you know, and I can plainly
       see
How much he knows about you—you can listen now to
       me:
He knows that you love ice cream—and vanilla is the
       best.
You don't like chocolate—that's okay—just save it for a
       guest.
He knows that pizza makes you smile each time you
       take a slice,

And second graders just like you think pepperoni's nice.
The thought that you do not believe in Santa is a shame
'Cause all the other boys and girls don't really feel the
      same.
I hope you'll never let my husband know the way you
      feel.
I've lived with him for years and I can promise you—
      he's real.
I promise he knows everything about good girls and
      boys,
Wherever they are in the world, so he can leave them
      toys.
The little elves who live with us all help him day and
      night
By working hard to make the toys for Santa in his flight.
You see how well he knows you, Ryan, how can it be
      true
That you're not sure about him—don't you know that he
      loves you?
I'll prove he's real, so just try this on Christmas eve this
      year:
Don't leave him milk and cookies, Ryan—that will make
      it clear:
Instead, on Christmas day, look for a treat meant just
      for you
That I will make while Santa's sleeping—here's a little
      clue:
It's white and smooth and very sweet and melts down
      when you bite.
Did you guess vanilla fudge, dear Ryan?
Why, yes, of course, you're right!

Most sincerely,
      Katarina Kringle

About the Author

Wilma has spent her life between South Florida and New York City. She attended Hunter College, married, raised her children, and worked as an executive legal secretary for a top Manhattan law firm. She began her writing with short stories, a few of which have been published and/or won prize money.

She has been living in North Florida since 1996, and continues to write short stories, poetry and memoirs. In 2006 she graduated to writing women's fiction and has just completed her fourth novel. Wilma is a member of The National League of American Pen Women and has an international byline.

Made in the USA
Charleston, SC
06 September 2013